DEC 1 0 2019

THE FORTY THIEVES

─◇─

Marjana's Tale

CHRISTY
LENZI

YELLOW
JACKET

For Noah and Joshua

YELLOW JACKET
an imprint of Little Bee Books

251 Park Avenue South, New York, NY 10010
Text copyright © 2019 by Christy Lenzi
All rights reserved, including the right of reproduction in whole or in part in any form.
Yellow Jacket and associated colophon are trademarks of Little Bee Books.
Manufactured in the United States of America MAP 1019
First Edition

10 9 8 7 6 5 4 3 2 1

Library of Congress Cataloging-in-Publication Data
Names: Lenzi, Christy, author.
Title: The forty thieves / by Christy Lenzi.
Description: First edition. | New York, NY: Yellow Jacket, [2019]
Summary: A loose retelling of Ali Baba and the Forty Thieves, set in tenth-century Baghdad, in which twelve-year-old Marjana tries to keep her brother, Jamal, from joining a gang while helping Ali Baba, their master's cruel brother. | Identifiers: LCCN 2019018448 (print) | LCCN 2019019973 (ebook) | Subjects: | CYAC: Brothers and sisters—Fiction. | Slavery—Fiction. | Gangs—Fiction. | Ali Baba (Legendary character)—Fiction. | Baghdad (Iraq)—History—10th century—Fiction. | Iraq—History—10th Century—Fiction. | BISAC: JUVENILE FICTION / Legends, Myths, Fables / General. | JUVENILE FICTION / Historical / Asia. | JUVENILE FICTION / Action & Adventure / General. | Classification: LCC PZ7.1.L445 (ebook) LCC PZ7.1.L445 For 2019
ISBN 978-1-4998-0945-9

yellowjacketreads.com

CHAPTER
1

The moon is a pearl against the black skin of night. I reach for it and sigh as I lie on my mat beneath the window. My little brother sighs, too. The snores of the nearby women and children drone in our ears like mosquitoes, but that's not what keeps us from sleep.

Jamal's nose almost touches mine. "I don't like when you wake me up with your dreams." His worry forms a line across the smooth surface of his forehead. "If the dreams are about Mother, then why do they make you cry?"

I draw in a deep breath. If only the scent of jasmine could fill me up like a bottle of perfume, I might not feel so hollow. "It's not the dreams that make me cry." I close my fingers over the moon until it disappears. "It's the waking."

"Marjana." He wiggles closer. "Tell me about Mother. How did our umi choose our names again?"

"Umi said she never would have believed that she would hold a treasure in her hands until the day she held me, so she gave me a name that means little pearl—her precious treasure." I roll the words over my tongue like savory morsels. "And you! You were such a dashing little fellow, she chose the name Jamal because it means handsome, of course."

"But what did Umi's name mean?"

I smile at the ceiling. "Wishes."

Jamal edges himself into the curve of my body. His skin smells of olive oil and goat's milk. "Tell me the twirling story," he whispers.

"Close your eyes, little donkey." I run my hands through his curly black hair. "I was just a twig of a girl—about seven years ago."

"How old?"

"I was . . ." Using my fingers, I count off seven from my twelve years. "Maybe five years old. And you were fat and round inside Umi's belly; she could barely hold the lute to play a song because you were in the way." I tickle him between the ribs to make him giggle.

"But one day Umi played the Twirling Song. She said if I spun around to the music, it would carry me to Allah, and when it stopped, His angels would fly me home. So Mother played the lute, and I twirled until all the colors of the world ran together. I spun until all the people, creatures, earth, and sky melted together into one beautiful, perfect paradise. When the music stopped, I fell to the floor, and the world kept spinning. Umi's laughter danced around and around with the colors until everything finally slowed down, and the angels brought me back home."

Jamal gazes at the ceiling, wide-eyed. "Magic," he whispers.

"No, not magic, Jamal. It was a sacred Sufi ritual. Umi's twirling was a way to feel closer to Allah."

"What's a—"

"Shh." I trace his profile with my fingertip. I didn't want to admit that I knew so little about Mother's beliefs, though I longed to. "That's my favorite memory of Umi."

Jamal's shoulders tense. "Why did our umi give us away?"

I sigh. I've explained hundreds of times. "You know that's not what happened. When she died, her master gave us to his sister and her husband as a wedding present. And you—a messy, stinky little boy. Not much of a wedding present." I dig my fingers into his side to make him smile again, but he shrugs my hands away.

"You should learn to play the Twirling Song on your lute, Marjana. Then I'll spin up to Allah and ask him to fly us both to Umi. Then you won't be so sad when you wake from your dreams."

A lump swells in my throat. "I can't."

"Why not?"

"I've forgotten the tune." I push him gently away and

rise from my mat. "I'm hungry. I'll go slice a pear for us." It hurts to think about the emptiness inside me that Jamal can see. I concentrate on stepping only on the patches of moonlight that slip through the openings in the carved window screens. I make it all the way to the cupboard without touching a single dark spot.

Finding a silver paring knife, I cut the skin from a pear in one long coil as a thrush sings a lonesome tune outside the harem walls. The ribbon of fruit skin drops to the table, and the birdsong ends, replaced with a new sound—a low rumble of thunder.

Impossible. The wet season won't come for months, and there's no smell of rain. Suddenly, little hairs on my arms stand up. The sound's not an approaching storm, but the thundering of many hoofbeats like an army galloping into battle. The noise grows louder. The pear slips from my fingers and rolls across the mosaic floor. My heart changes its rhythm like a drum banging out a warning. Hoofbeats rumble in my chest and under my feet. When the knife shakes in my trembling fingers, I clutch it so tightly my knuckles turn white. It's as if the wind of fate is hurtling toward me like a sandstorm.

The storm of hoofbeats roars right up to the house.

My heart pounds against my rib cage, trying to escape.

With a sound like a thunderclap, doors crack and rip off their hinges. An army of men on horses crashes into the house with gleaming scimitars.

I scream, frozen in place. Other screams pierce the air as the sleepers in the harem wake to a nightmare. Slave women grab their children. Mistress and her little niece and nephew clutch each other, their eyes wide with terror. Jamal's face turns pale as a leper's.

A tall, thin man with a long dark beard and a face as cold as the devil's rides up the front steps and through the doorway. His stallion rears and snorts, nostrils flaring.

A chill shoots down my spine.

Master's away on a journey, but his eunuch khādim guards rush in, swords drawn.

They're outnumbered.

The captain, this devil-man, spurs his horse and charges at their leader.

I scream, turning away, but the *thwack* of the man's scimitar says the guard is dead. Mistress sobs as the men crash through the house, grabbing silver, gold, anything valuable. The women scream and try to hide the children as riders whisk people onto their horses—they're taking Mistress's niece and nephew along with the slaves.

Cook grabs my arm, trying to pull me under the table to safety. *Jamal.* My brother's a stone statue, standing on his mat in the moonlight, miles and miles away.

"Jamal!" I struggle free from her grasp and run toward him, but it's like I'm moving through deep water. *Faster*, I order my legs. But I'm too late—one of the riders snatches Jamal and pulls the horse's reins around to gallop away. I rush at the rider and beat his legs with my fists, forgetting I still have the small knife in my hand.

A strong arm hooks my waist, jerking me upward. The devil-man.

I kick and fight against his hold, but his arms are like metal bindings. I bite him hard, but he thrusts me into the saddle in front of him and locks me in a tight grip. I struggle to turn and see Jamal, but the man raises his fist in the air, shouts to his men, and spurs his horse toward the door. With a jolt, they burst out of Master's house into the night.

CHAPTER

2

Hoofbeats and wild shrieking fill the air as the riders thunder toward the Basra gate. The gate guardians are no match for the thieves, who overpower them and open the heavy iron double doors of the inner wall and then the outer. In moments, we're galloping out of the city, over the moat, and into the darkness surrounding Baghdad. At first, I can only scream. The gold rings on the man's bare arms cut into my ribs. The hard edge of the saddle presses into my thighs as I'm thrust forward with every stride of the horse. But after a while, my throat grows raw and my body stiffens against the pain.

A tattoo of a green serpent curls around the devil-man's

arm, baring its fangs at me. I swear its eyes flash red for a moment in the darkness, but that's impossible. As if in a trance, I stare at the blade of the paring knife still in my hand, hidden by folds of my qamis. I could plunge the blade into the man's thigh and leap from the horse to escape, but I'd lose my chance to save Jamal. I inch the knife up until the blade's hidden in my fist, the handle concealed beneath my sleeve.

The riders finally halt at a cedar grove where a man with a drove of mules waits. My body has turned so numb, I can barely move. The riders dismount to rearrange their plunder onto the backs of the mules and tie up the captives. I strain to catch sight of Jamal in the darkness among the blur of people and horses, but the devil-man forces my arms behind my back to bind them.

I hold my breath and clasp my hands together, hoping he won't discover the knife, but he winds the rope around my wrists without hesitating. He turns me around and stands, looking at me in silence for a moment, his back to the moonlight. His face is in shadow, but he can see me plainly enough.

I long for my gauzy headscarf. I like to let it "acciden-tally" fall over my face like a wealthy woman's veil so people can't see my eyes. Umi used to say my green eyes were beautiful, like sparkling gemstones. But eyes reveal too much. I don't want people to see what I'm thinking or know what I'm feeling.

The devil-man touches my cheek. His nails are long like a cat's claws. He runs his finger down the side of my face and lifts my chin. It reminds me of the way Mistress's cat plays with the mice it catches before killing them. The thought makes me wince, but I stand tall and straight, facing him. The tattooed serpent's body winds all the way up his arm and coils over his chest. Instead of a tail, the serpent has another head, even fiercer than the first, with fire erupting from its mouth. As the man's chest rises and falls with his breath, the serpent undulates back and forth, as if it is preparing to strike me.

The captain turns and calls to the man in charge of the

mules, who lifts me onto one of the animals. After all the plunder is secured, we're off again, headed in the direction of Basra, a seaport trading town Jamal and I have been to before with Master and Mistress. The cold desert air seeps all the life from my bones. Before long, I drift in and out of sleep.

I wake sometime later to the sounds of the men calling to each other. I glance around. The full moon has vanished, but the sky's getting lighter in the east. Though it's still dark, I see the riders more clearly now. They point to an oasis of date palm trees up ahead as they talk. The men are all bare-chested and tattooed. Gold and silver earrings, necklaces, and arm rings glitter against their skin. Their turbans shine a brilliant white.

The men will surely sell the captives as soon as we get to Basra. My breath catches in my throat. Jamal might be taken from me and sent far away where I'll never find him.

The riders direct their horses toward the palm trees

and soon dismount and stretch. I ache to do the same. Rough hands lift me from the mule and set me on the ground. The men do the same to the other captives. The prisoners' faces are ashen, everyone wearing the same stricken expression of a person waking from a night-mare—unsure of what's real and what's not.

Jamal calls out to me, his voice cracked and small, like a broken hand bell. I push over to him, and he falls across my lap, curling himself around my knees. "Mar-jana, they made the guard's blood spill out on the floor," he whispers. His thin body grows taut like a bowstring. I wish I could place my finger over his trembling lips, rest my hand on his head, and smooth his wild hair, his wild thoughts.

"I know. But they won't do that to us, Jamal. We'll be all right."

"How do you know?" His voice is the squeak of a mouse.

"We're valuable, like the gold and silver around their necks. They wear them proud as peacocks, see? We're treasure, Jamal." I give a little laugh. "A dirty runt like you—not much of a treasure if you ask me, but this pig-headed captain of the thieves won't listen to me. He seems to think you're quite a prize." I glance at the devil-man who stands with his arms crossed over his chest, surveying the plunder.

Jamal's lips tighten into a small grin. "Will they take us to a magic palace?"

"Magic palace?"

"They have magic, Marjana. When they stopped to load the mules, I saw one of them say a strange word and then open a little wooden chest, the size of Mistress's jewelry box. He pulled out enough food to feed all the men. And not pan bread—banquet food, like Master eats. Whole roasted hens! Melons, figs, and cheese. Cakes and goblets of juice! All for just a quick snack, too. They didn't even take many bites of it and just left the rest on the ground."

He must be dizzy with hunger and imagining things. Jamal is always looking for magic, like the kind you hear about in tall tales. I pretend to carefully consider his words as I strain my ears to listen to the captain. He's ordering his men to plunge the captives in the stream to scrub them and have them dressed in clean clothes. The looming slave market makes my stomach churn, but I tilt my head and look thoughtful for Jamal. "Well, I'm not sure about taking us to a magic palace. It's hard to know. They certainly seem to like gold and silver. They may decide they want to trade some treasure."

"Trade treasure?"

"Well, a boy like you might get them some valuable jewelry in trade at the market. I bet that thought has crossed their greedy little minds. Look how they show off their pretty arm rings, strutting around like roosters." I wet my lips. "But the thing about being traded is . . . well, we want to be traded *together*."

Jamal sits up. "They might trade me without you?" His mouth falls open.

I shrug my shoulders, trying to appear unconcerned. "Those men don't look very smart. You and I go together. Like a pair of earrings. We're too valuable to be separated, but they might be too stupid to think of keeping us together how we belong. Fortunately, I've already thought of that."

As I speak, I edge up to the palm tree until it almost touches my tied wrists. Opening my fist, I let the knife slip to the ground near the trunk behind my back and cover it quickly with sand as best I can. "I won't let them separate us." I lower my voice as one of the men approaches to make us start washing up. "Don't worry, Jamal. I have a plan."

3

The water feels cool on my feet. I hug myself to cover my chest and crouch down, wishing there were more water in the stream to cover me. Even though my body hasn't changed from a girl's to a woman's yet, I no longer feel like a child and the thought of washing like this out in the open makes me wish I were invisible. But the thieves don't seem to notice or care. To them I'm just a slave— property, a creature without feelings. The man roughly scrubs my skin with sand and a horse brush, bringing tears to my eyes, and then pours a bucket of water over my head to rinse me off.

Some of the men stand posted around the grove to

watch for any approaching parties, but most of the others have fallen asleep leaning against palm trees or lying in the sand. I count forty men in all, including the captain.

After Jamal and I dress in clean clothes and I put on the red headscarf I've been given, the man ties our wrists behind our backs again and tells us to return to the tree and sleep. Now's the time to dig up my knife. I'll keep it hidden in my sleeve so I'll be ready to cut our ropes and escape with Jamal. I don't like thinking of the men who are keeping watch. But they'll be on the look-out for intruders, not escaping children. Besides, the men won't harm the captives—it would decrease their value at the slave market. At least I *hope* they won't.

I head back to the tree, but stop mid-stride. My heart almost stops as well. The devil-man's walking toward the very tree where I buried the knife. I glance at the spot and almost choke on the breath that catches in my throat. The silver tip of the knife blade's sticking up through the sand. Sunlight glints off it like a sparkling diamond.

I bite my lip and walk quickly toward the tree with Jamal as I watch the devil-man. He doesn't seem to notice us, so I pull Jamal down with me to the ground to wait, several feet away.

The captain unwinds part of his turban cloth and dabs the sweat on his forehead. He looks as if he might sit down to rest, too, but then he stops. His body straightens. He's seen it.

I hold my breath.

He bends down and plucks the knife from its pitiful hiding spot. After turning it over in his hands several times, he slips it into the sash at his waist and sits down with his legs crossed. He places the end of his turban cloth over his eyes and leans back against the tree to sleep.

I sigh and let my head fall to the ground. No knife, no escape. I, too, close my eyes so Jamal won't see the tears rising in them. I stay silent for a long time, until I feel a tickling in my ear as Jamal whispers, "Marjana, what's your plan?" His eyes are bright. When his face is clean and his hair shines, he looks like a little prince. He'll certainly be one of the first children sold at the slave market in the morning.

The devil-man snores quietly.

Staring at the tip of the silver knife handle poking out of his sash, I whisper back, "It's a very tricky plan, Jamal. I need lots of help. Lots of wishes."

"I can wish for you."

"Then lie here as still as you can. Now close your eyes and think of our umi—"

"Umi, Umi, Umi—"

"Shh. Say it in your head."

His lips move as he thinks of Mother.

"And wish with all your might for my plan to work until I come back."

Jamal's eyes pop open. "Where are you going?"

"Shh. Just concentrate on your wishes, Jamal. I'll be back in a moment." I glance around. The guards at their posts have their faces turned away from us, and all the men nearby are sleeping. I look at the other children and feel a pang of regret—when Mother died and we were sent to Master's household, I snapped shut and built a thick wall around myself like an oyster builds its shell around a pearl. I never let anyone get close to me, even the girls my age. It would be nice to have a friend right now.

They all stand huddled together in small groups like sheep. I try to get their attention to show them that I have a plan, but when they see me gesturing with my bound hands, they look so frightened. They glance nervously at the men and shake their heads at me. They don't want to risk trying to escape. But I can't let these men lead me and Jamal off to market, where who knows what will become of us. *Never.* As quietly as possible, I push myself to my knees and move closer to the devil-man. I stop and look around. No one's watching me. I rise and move even closer, until I'm by his side, almost touching him.

The green serpent glares at me, daring me to come any closer. The man's loose headcloth covers his eyes and nose, and his beard hides most of his mouth, but even the fierce set of his jaw makes me tremble. The knife handle is in easy reach, but with my hands tied behind my back, I'll have to twist around and slip it from his sash without seeing what I'm doing.

Umi, Umi, Umi, I chant inside my head as if the thought of Mother might somehow give me the power to free myself and Jamal. I glance around one last time, lick my lips, and stretch my fingers out for the knife. His silken sash brushes against my skin, and I freeze. But my touch wasn't heavy enough to disturb the devil-man. I try again. The shock of the cool silver handle assures my fingers, and I slide them around the hilt.

The man's snores continue—no one's noticed me. I pull on the knife. It slides partly out of the sash, but in order to draw it completely free, I'll have to move forward on my knees, away from him a little as I tug. My hands are sweaty now. If I fumble, he might wake thinking I'm attacking him and he'll defend himself. I swallow with difficulty and steady my grip.

Umi, Umi, Umi.

I move forward as I pull, and the knife slips free of the sash. As the weight of it lifts from his waist, the devil-man stops snoring.

I forget how to breathe.

"Captain!" Shouts erupt from the guards. *They've seen me?*

My heart races. I drop the knife behind me and crumple to the ground, bracing myself for the strike of the man's blade on the back of my neck.

"Captain, they're coming!"

The devil-man leaps to his feet and draws his scimitar.

"Arise!" he shouts. "Mount!"

The men spring into action the moment the words leave his mouth. He points his weapon.

Shaking, I lift my eyes and follow the tip of the scimitar. I stare past the palm trees to the desert at what looks like a dust storm coming from the direction we traveled the night before.

"Attack!"

The men thunder by me on their horses. The devil-man, too, jumps on his stallion and races away, toward the dust cloud.

"Marjana, how did you do that?" Jamal's eyebrows slide to the top of his forehead. "That was strong magic. It made them all go away!"

The dust cloud must be men who have gathered to catch the thieves. Perhaps they'll defeat the robbers and rescue us. But perhaps they won't. This moment could be our only hope.

"They may return, Jamal. Let's hurry." I rock back and forth, moving the blade across Jamal's ropes. As I work, battle noises rise in the distance.

All the huddled children wear a new look on their faces: hope. They won't want to risk escaping with us now that they might be saved by the approaching men. *Am I doing the right thing?* We might find ourselves sleeping safely on our mats the next evening if we just stay here with them and see what happens. The wind of fate whispers in my ear and tugs my fingers until the blade severs the final thread.

"We're free, Jamal," I say when he finishes cutting through my bonds. The words sound strange and beautiful, like music sung in a foreign language.

I run to the group of huddled children and begin cutting the binds of a wide-eyed girl—Mistress's niece. But before I've barely begun to fray the rope, the sound of hooves thunders closer. We can't afford to stay and help—if the thieves have won the battle, they'll just capture us again. I place the knife in the girl's palm and wrap her fingers around the hilt and squeeze her hand.

"May Allah protect you," I whisper.

"They're coming this way, Jamal! We have to leave. Now!" I untie a mule that still has jugs of water slung over its back and hoist my brother up, and then I pull myself up behind him. I tuck my heels into the mule's sides to make it sprint forward and then we're off.

"Let's go home!" I cry as we gallop in the direction of Baghdad.

CHAPTER
4

Jamal names the mule Batal, Hero, for carrying us away from the devil-man and having jugs of water on his back to keep us from dying of thirst. After riding Batal for hours and hours under the blazing sun, the image of the great round city of Baghdad in the distance is like a shimmering mirage. I sigh in relief. We'll make it before sunset, when the heavy gates close against outsiders for the night.

By the time the sun sinks low in the sky, we cross the bridge of the first canal and can see the city in all its glory, nestled like a beautiful pendant on the silver thread of the Tigris River, the brilliant white dome of the Taj Palace shining like a diamond in its center. Home. At least, the only home we have known.

Batal the mule picks up his weary pace to a trot as we enter the city gates. The narrow streets are emptying as people hurry to get to their destinations before Maghrib, sunset prayers. We arrive at the damaged front doors of Master's house in the falling dark, just as the muezzin gives his call to prayer from the minaret near the mosque.

Jamal, sleepy from the journey, mumbles, "Won't Master and Mistress be so pleased to see us? They probably thought they'd never see us again. I can't wait to tell Cook about the captain and the thieves, and their magic banquet, and the story of our brave escape!"

A lump forms in my throat when I think of the other slaves and Mistress's niece and nephew. "Jamal, it was exciting to escape, and we are happy to be safe, but Master and Mistress will not be as happy as you think. After all, we are only two slaves, but they've lost family to the thieves and many valuables.

Jamal yawns. "Let's go inside, Marjana. I want to drink

a hundred jugs of water and eat a thousand of Cook's cakes and then go to sleep for a million years."

— ◈ —

I was right about Master and Mistress not being as happy as Jamal had imagined when we returned without Mistress's family members. Mistress wept and shook for weeks afterward, and Master, always grumpy, was furious with his material losses and cursed and grumbled for days.

But Jamal and I are together and safe now. Who would believe that we escaped the infamous Forty Thieves? I hardly believe it myself, even though a month of days and nights have passed since we returned. Sometimes, I lie awake on my mat at night and think of Mistress's niece with the wide eyes, wrapping her fingers around the paring knife I'd put in her hands. She and the rest of the captives have probably been sold in Basra by now. Who knows what their fates will hold for them?

When the events of that day seem more like a nightmare that I must have dreamed, I go to the kitchen and find a paring knife like the one I had that day. I turn it over in my hands and feel the weight of it. I slide my finger over the blade to feel the coolness of it on my skin, and I remember how it felt to cut Jamal and myself free of our bindings. Then it all feels real and I know I would do it again if I had to.

I don't think I will ever feel safe now, knowing the devil-man is out there. I still have flashbacks of the captain's green serpent tattoo curled around his arm. But Jamal has forgotten his fear and remembers only the glory of escaping.

I pull my scarf over my face as we hurry to the main part of the house. We've been summoned. Master and his brother, Ali Baba, sit on a mountain of cushions. Master, large and portly, sprawls over the pillows and smokes a hookah. As he sucks the cooled smoke through the hose, the water in the vase bubbles. He doesn't acknowledge us as we stand in the doorway, so we wait quietly to be addressed.

Ali Baba, a tiny man wearing ragged clothes, smiles

kindly at us. He's a woodcutter, living in poverty with his wife, Leila, and their grown son, who is said to be a layabout, refusing to accompany his father on his daily trek to the woods.

Ali Baba continues his conversation with Master. "Yes, Cassim, it's a terrible thing that the thieves stole so much from your house, but praise Allah, you and your wife are safe and your shop stayed secure."

Master is a clever merchant of the most expensive, sought-after items. He buys beautiful, dark-wooden furniture inlaid with precious ivory and mother-of-pearl from craftsmen in the Maghreb, and giant bronze and copper engraved items—teapots and hookahs taller than I—from Iran, and sells them at exorbitant prices to the wealthy families of Baghdad.

"Thankfully," Ali Baba says, "your shop hasn't been broken into by the child street gangs, as so many others have been lately."

Beside me, Jamal catches his breath. He listens with interest as Ali Baba talks about the gangs.

"It's a shame so many desperate souls in Baghdad suffer from such poverty that they turn to crime."

"Bah!" Master lets out a disdainful laugh. "They turn to crime because they're lazy and bored. If any of those brats try to break into my shop, I'll show them suffering!"

Jamal snickers. The men don't hear him, but it makes me nervous. I pinch his arm to hush him. His disruption isn't the only thing that worries me. Sometimes when Jamal's chores are done, and I'm still working, he slips away from the house. He won't tell me where he's been, but the gleam in his eyes when he returns, dirty and rumpled, makes me anxious. Mother would have been able to keep him from searching out these gangs he's always chattering about, but what can I do?

Ali Baba sighs. "Most are just poor, hungry street urchins without any families. May Allah have mercy on them."

"Humph." Master blows smoke out in ring-shaped puffs that float toward us like little clouds. Jamal reaches for one. I stiffen. When will he behave? Master's eyes narrow.

He hands the hookah to Ali Baba and struggles to his feet.

"There has been no music in the house this past month." He glares at me and Jamal as if it were our fault that my lute and his drum were destroyed in the attack. "Evenings are too dull without music and dancing. I've replaced your instruments. You will begin practicing again first thing tomorrow morn—"

"But—"

Master frowns at my interruption.

I don't say what I'm thinking: that while I'd love to play my lute first thing in the morning, Mistress has already made plans to go to the baths at daybreak and I must accompany her.

His face hardens. "What's the meaning of this?" He gestures at my scarf—I've forgotten to push it back. "No slave girl of mine shall wear a veil. Who do you think you are?"

He tears the scarf away, examining me like he

examines his hookah to make sure it works properly.

I flinch, but stare straight back.

"How dare you defy me with those eyes of yours!" Master slaps me, stinging my cheek. I force myself to look at the floor.

Ali Baba stands. "Brother, remember Allah is merciful."

Master grunts. "I am not Allah."

Jamal's fists tighten into balls. Before I can stop him, he springs at Master, kicking his shin and punching him in the gut. I hurry over and grab Jamal away. Will he be beaten?

Master turns and, to my surprise, slaps me a second time.

"Control him, or you'll be whipped." He returns to his hookah, dismissing us. My face burns fire, but his coldness hardens my heart to ice.

After we finish work and are sent to bed, we find a lute, a pipe, and a tabor on our mats. Jamal smiles, but tears fill my eyes. I cradle the curves of the lute and rest my head on the instrument's neck, breathing in its warm scent of leather and wood. It's just like the lute Mother played when she was still alive.

When I wake, I have ridges on my cheek from the strings. On my other cheek, the print of Master's hand still burns.

— ◈ —

"Magical stories for a dirham!"

I step around the old storyteller calling out his wares and peer around the baskets I carry as I scurry after Mistress through the busy streets of the city. Children watching a shadow play performed in front of the butcher's shop laugh and shout, bumping into me as I try to pass them. People flood the bazaar, making it difficult to keep sight of Mistress's billowing veil and large, swaying backside.

Cries of merchants and the smell of raw meat and spices—saffron, cinnamon, cardamom—fill the air. During the final days of Ramadan, people are preparing for Eid al-Fitr, the feast to end their month-long fast. In the past, we would never have seen the kinds of street performers we see now, especially during such a holy month, but men say the government's control has weakened and now tricksters work freely in public, hoping to draw in the many foreigners of other religions who now flock to the city. "Preachers" conjure water into milk or pick an apple from empty air for their audience. Some, with their booths covered in mystical signs, feature poltergeists and perform exorcisms for a fee. Others juggle snakes and promise fire-walking later this afternoon. Some people, like Master, don't seem to mind the loosened state of affairs, but other, more devoted Muslims grumble nervously under their breath.

Dodging street performers and beggars, I manage to catch up to Mistress and her sister-in-law as they arrive at the steps of the women's public bathhouse.

Mistress is already giving orders. "Try to find me the bath attendant named Saja, Marjana. Leila says the girl knows the best perfume recipes and has the hands of an angel."

Leila smiles. "It's true—she has a gift."

Mistress clutches her sister-in-law's arm. "Last time, my usual girl almost broke my fingers and spine when she cracked my joints. She nearly ripped the skin off my back with her scourging." She breathes heavily as she lumbers up the bathhouse steps. "You know how delicate I am."

I try not to smile at my disagreeable mistress. "Yes, of course."

Steam pours from the arched entrance of the stone building as we open the door. Pausing at the threshold, Mistress and Leila utter a quick prayer of protection against harmful beings. The baths are supposedly a resort of evil jinn, but Master doesn't seem afraid of them. I'm not sure anymore what I think. I want to be a devout Muslim like Umi was, but sometimes it's hard to believe in things that I can't see or touch. Even Allah sometimes seems like a misty figment of my imagination, and I wonder if my prayers really ever reach His ears or if I am praying to the wind.

We remove our sandals to the shock of cool marble. Figures appear and disappear through thick curtains of steam. Voices murmur in the mist, echoing off the mosaic walls. It would be difficult to tell whether they are the whisperings of bath patrons or jinn. The fragrance of chamomile and peppermint oils fills the air as I help the women undress near the hot, bubbly fountain and soothing water of the pool.

While Mistress and Leila soak in the warm water, I leave to find Saja. A girl stands near the bubbling fountain; her dark braid hangs down her bare back and sways between her shoulder blades as she folds linens.

"As-salaam alaykum. I am looking for Saja."

"Wa alaykum as-salaam. I am Saja."

The girl's face is flushed from the steam, but I can tell she's been crying by the redness in her eyes. I start to reach out and touch her arm, but I draw my hand back. "I'm Marjana," I say. "My mistress would like your assistance."

Instead of answering, Saja closes her eyes and draws in a slow, deep breath.

I raise my voice. "Please come with—"

"Freshly picked jasmine." Saja opens her eyes.

"What?" My fingers move to my sash, where I had slipped a sprig of jasmine while leaving the house that morning.

"It suits you so much better than the musky ambergris that most slave girls wear." The girl smiles and takes my wrist, touching it gently at my pulse. "If you crush the blossoms against your skin right here—"

I slip my hand away, not used to being touched.

Saja blinks. She turns to gather her linens, but starts sniffling again and looks as if she might start crying. "I'm sorry," she whispers. "It's just that I can't stop thinking about my little brother; he works in the men's bathhouse. He got caught stealing from the bath patrons this morning, and the master of the baths whipped him." She wipes her eyes. "His back is covered in welts."

I wince, imagining Master whipping little Jamal like that.

She stands up straighter, and seems to pull herself together. "I won't burden you with my troubles." She points to my sash where the jasmine is hidden. "If you bring me a basketful of blossoms, I can press them for jasmine oil and mix it with powdered orris root."

"Why?"

"I just thought you might like to have some jasmine perfume made from the flowers you like so well. And I enjoy creating the potions. Kadira, the woman who runs the apothecary shop with her brother, taught me how to mix them."

I start to say I need to get back to Mistress, but Saja keeps on talking, making excited gestures with her hands as she speaks.

"When I was young, Kadira noticed on her visits to the baths that I was interested in scents and could discern which elements had gone into all her perfumes. It wasn't long before I was helping her form new recipes, and she kept leaving me plants and oils to make my own and seeds to grow the plants myself! Now I—"

"I understand," I interrupt. I don't know how to talk with someone like Saja. She's too open with strangers. I'm afraid she might expect me to be the same way in return. "You'll get your jasmine." When I see the hurt look on Saja's face, something inside me wavers like a lute string plucked out of tune. Unsure of what to say, I glance over my shoulder. "My mistress is waiting."

CHAPTER

5

On the next bath day, I rise early in order to pick enough jasmine petals to fill a basket. It will be easy enough to hide it among the bundles of linens, jars of henna, and my lute. Mistress asked me to play some soothing music while they recline at the baths. I've been practicing every chance I get. The melodies that find their way from my fingers to the strings are different from the ones I used to play before that day the Forty Thieves came. Something about that day—the horrible possibility of losing Jamal and the thrill of freedom when we escaped—stirs my heart and wants to find its way out in my music.

Jamal's already been playing the drum for years, and

Mistress is delighted with his progress on the pipe—she says he plays like a snake charmer. But practicing the pipe and assisting Cook aren't enough to keep Jamal out of trouble.

Just the previous morning, Jamal took the labels off Cook's spice jars and switched them around without her knowing. As if that weren't enough, he'd laughed out loud watching Master clutch his throat and shout after taking a bite of pears with hot pepper sprinkled on them instead of cinnamon. I rub the bruise on my cheek where Master punished me for Jamal's mischief.

As soon as I settle Mistress and her sister-in-law by the pool, I hurry to find Saja, but Saja finds me first.

"As-salaam alaykum, Marjana." She takes hold of my hand, her eyes swollen, again.

I stare at Saja's fingers caging mine and resist the urge to peel them away. "Here are the flowers you asked for." I hand her the basket of sweet-smelling jasmine blossoms and turn to go. "My mistress is waiting for us."

"Wait, Marjana. My brother—"

I'm afraid the girl might cry again, but I find myself hesitating to listen. Something about the tone of Saja's voice echoes the anxiety I have for my own brother.

Saja whispers, "Badi's in even deeper trouble, now."

"He got caught stealing again?" I don't mean to ask the question, but it slips out.

"No, it's not that. The master beat him so hard last time, he hasn't done it since. This is worse. Some of the older boys took Badi into their gang. He's a street warrior now." She sniffles and blows her nose on one of the bath linens.

My heart skips a beat. "But that's not real warfare, is it? It's just a boys' game." I try to make my voice light, but I can't help thinking of the street gangs Ali Baba talked about and the gleam in Jamal's eyes.

"No, I've seen them outside the bathhouse at night sometimes. They weave helmets and shields for their leaders and ride on each other like warriors on horses."

"See—it's just pretend."

"They have weapons! They make battles with the other

43

street gangs at night and break into shops. Badi could grow up to become a bloodthirsty thief and join that gang of robbers everyone talks about."

My skin prickles. "The Forty Thieves?"

Saja nods. "People see them sometimes, outside the city."

The devil-man, so nearby—my heart beats faster. "You're right—you can't let that happen."

"Are you all right, Marjana? You've turned pale. Are the jinn affecting you?"

"I'm fine." I take a deep breath. "You're right. The Forty Thieves were young boys once. You can't let your brother become like them. Can you leave the bathhouse at all? Maybe you could bring Badi with you to my master's slave quarters sometime—I have a brother, too. Maybe they just need someone to play with in a safe, proper place out of the streets, to keep them out of trouble."

Saja's face lights up as if I've offered her the royal Taj Palace. "Well, I haven't been out very often and don't know my way around the city. The mistress of the baths is a monster and easily annoyed. Some of the girls bribe the khādim or sneak out of the bathhouse through a broken shutter when their work is done, but I've never—"

I turn to go. "Well, I understand. My mistress is waiting for us."

"Wait!" Saja catches up with me. "I want to." She blinks at the mosaic floor, looking surprised at herself. "And I'll take Badi this evening if you tell me how to get there." She beams. "Oh, thank you! I'm so glad you came today—I hardly knew what to do."

The heat and steam make it difficult to breathe normally. Saja's nearness is smothering me. I take the linens from her. "We should go to Mistress."

Saja smiles, grabs my hand, and practically drags me through the steam to where Mistress reclines on her mat beside the pool, munching dried jujubes. Leila's in the pool; when she sees us, hand in hand, she sighs and says to Mistress, "Oh, seeing these two together reminds me of my days as a girl in Iran before I was given in marriage to Ali Baba and came to Baghdad. How I miss my soul sister."

As Saja begins loosening Mistress's pinned-up hair and applying the henna, I sit cross-legged on the floor watching with my lute in my lap. I don't know what Leila means by "soul sister." I run my fingers over the fine wood of my new lute. Its smooth curves and delicate strings send that old familiar thrill through me. As Saja works the muddy green paste into Mistress's hair, I strum the song I've been working on.

Mistress closes her eyes and asks Leila the very question I'm wondering: "What are soul sisters?"

Leila rests her arms over the tiled edge of the pool. "Oh, the closest friends in the world." Her eyes light up. "When a young woman finds her soul sister, they take a vow together at a shrine in front of their family and friends." Leila's happy voice seems to dance to the music of the lute.

I've never heard of a vow like that. I can't imagine

having such a close friend that I would want to make a vow to her.

"A matchmaker arranges it by sending a wax doll to the girl. If she says no, it's returned with a black veil, but if the proposal is accepted, it's returned with a necklace around its head like a crown."

Mistress makes a hissing sound through her teeth. "Sounds like a marriage. Except for the most important thing—the dowry." Mistress lowers her voice. "My husband would call such women 'witches,' I'm sure." She giggles.

"Oh, but it's a most holy vow of friendship, honored by the whole community. Soul sisters know each other better than anyone else. They share even their most secret thoughts." Leila smiles as if that's a good thing.

I'd rather be slashed with a knife than have my thoughts opened for someone to see.

Leila sighs. "My soul sister used to send me kitchen supplies."

"Kitchen supplies?" Mistress snorts. "My husband sent me far better gifts than that. Once he gave me a beautiful little dagger made of silver, with a hidden compartment in the hilt."

"Oh, but sister-in-law, these were special gifts, full of meaning. A cinnamon stick was not just a cinnamon stick. It meant 'I trust you.' A whole cardamom said, 'You are my secret-keeper,' and a cracked one meant she was in agony." Leila smiles. "My favorite, the tiny sesame seed, said, 'You are my treasure,' but the pear seed . . ." She swallows hard and stares at the pattern on the floor where she sits. "The pear seed . . ."

Mistress raises her head. The green henna in her hair makes her look like an evil demon. "Well, what does the pear seed mean?"

Leila dabs at the tears welling up in her eyes and whispers, "It means 'I hate you.'"

CHAPTER

6

I hate you.

My fingers fumble on the lute strings when Leila tells us the meaning of her soul sister's pear-seed gift. The notes I'm playing clash together. Saja glances in my direction. I almost pull down my scarf, but Saja acts as if my eyes are like pleasant pools rather than locked doors to be broken into.

Mistress frowns at her sister-in-law and lies back down. "Then why on earth would she ever give you a pear seed? Sounds like your soul sister's love was not as strong as you say."

Leila's silent as she traces the colorful pattern in the tiles. After a few moments, she says quietly, "Nay, you're wrong. Sometimes love is so strong, it makes us weak. When my father promised me in marriage to Ali Baba, and I told her I must move away, she broke our vow of sisterhood and said she never wanted to see me again."

Saja wipes the henna from her hands and takes Leila's hand in hers, massaging the woman's fingers. Leila blinks back tears.

"Please—tell us about your home country." Saja surprises us all by speaking. "Was it beautiful?"

Leila smiles. She seems grateful to Saja for changing the subject. "Oh yes! When I was a girl, we lived by the Khazar Sea, the loveliest place in the world. The water sparkled like diamonds and emeralds tossed in a silver bowl. Have you ever seen the sea?"

Saja shakes her head. "No, but I can imagine the water—it sounds like the color of Marjana's eyes."

The women turn to look at me. No one has said such a kind thing about me since Umi died. A warm sensation creeps up my neck and over my cheeks as I play.

"Ah, I think you're right." Leila smiles and pats Saja's hand as she steps out of the pool. She dries herself off, dresses, and gathers her soaps and linens. "And now I must go home to my son, Rasheed. As-salaam alaykum."

When Leila leaves, Saja wraps Mistress's hair in linen and massages her muscles. After a few moments, Mistress's snoring grows louder than the lute, and I set it aside. Saja whispers, "Your turn."

I've been looking forward to this. The water's so inviting. I slip off my qamis and sirwal and slide into the bubbling pool, letting myself sink to the bottom like a stone. The roiling liquid pulses over me, washing away the grime, the streets, the masters, the thieves—the whole world—and wraps me in a blanket of peace.

As I soak, Saja spreads a piece of linen over her white attendant's skirt and mixes more henna. When I step out of the pool, Saja beckons me to her side where she sits cross-legged on the floor, and I lie down next to her and rest my head in her lap. The henna paste smells sweet.

Saja works it gingerly into my hair, humming my lute tune. Her voice makes me think of warm honey, but it doesn't melt the stiffness in my bones.

Saja pauses for a moment. "Where did you learn that song for your lute, Marjana? It sounds . . . lonely. Like the music wants to be known and heard by someone who understands it or it will die of heartache." Saja sighs. "I know what that feels like."

No one's ever talked about my music that way before. It's as if Saja has peeked inside the window of my heart, a window I keep locked up with a wooden screen. "I made it up myself."

"It's lovely," Saja whispers, rinsing her hands. She kneels beside me on a cushion and rubs perfumed oils over my body in gentle waves of pressure. "You have such hard knots in your muscles, Marjana. Relax."

But Saja's words only make my body tense up, resisting her soothing fingers.

"This is violet oil. Violets are the trickiest flowers—

their scent is so difficult to capture and keep. They refuse to be held for more than a moment. Take a deep breath."

I inhale the sweet smell.

"Burnt sugar and lemons—that's what violets smell like, don't they. But now take another breath."

I inhale again, but smell nothing.

Saja laughs. "Gone! Coy little things. Soon you'll smell their sweetness again."

Saja's right. The next time I take a breath, there it is, like magic. As she works, Saja talks about everything under the sun, whispering so she won't wake Mistress. She speaks of flowers, herbs, and spices as though they're characters living in a story.

Then she lowers her voice even more. "Marjana, I'll tell you a secret I haven't told anyone else. I once had a dream I'll never forget. It's not a grand dream about living in a palace or finding a treasure, but I think about it all the time. I wish for it to come true. Sometimes, I tell myself the dream, like a story, over and over, as if that will make it real."

I'm reminded of how I sometimes do the same thing with my dreams about Umi coming back to be with me and Jamal and being a family again. I wait, curious to hear Saja's wish.

"One day I dreamed that I was free and owned my own perfume shop. Me! And all day long I worked with the most beautiful smells on earth—rose, sandalwood, vanilla, cedar, apple, lily of the valley. . . . I made perfumes that captured every beautiful scent in the world—scents that held people's best memories. When customers bought my perfumes, the scents made them happy because they were reminded of their favorite things—a childhood joy, a lover's embrace, a friend's smile, or perhaps a mother's voice." Saja sighed. "I think of this dream all the time."

I see Saja's dream as vividly as if I'd dreamed it myself. My body relaxes a little, and some of the tension dissolves. I listen in a trance to her words, unused to conversations that don't involve orders or complaints, until Mistress finally wakes with a start. The woman immediately begins giving commands, breaking the peaceful spell Saja created.

"Oh, we must hurry!" Mistress scrambles to gather her things. "Marjana, as soon as we get home, you and Jamal shall put the house in order. Cut some gillyflowers, bring out the gold-fringed cushions, and assist Cook. My husband has a guest tonight—the fortune-teller, Abu-Zayed."

Saja gives me a nervous glance as she hands me the lute. Fortune-telling is black magic—Sihr. It's thought that harmful jinn creep up to the lowest heaven to eavesdrop on the angels' conversations and carry the information to fortune-tellers' ears. Umi once told me that shooting stars are really balls of fire that angry angels hurl at the retreating jinn.

Mistress's news doesn't surprise me; Master isn't pious like most Muslims, and he looks down on his devout brother, Ali Baba. Ali Baba and his family are Sufis like Umi was, Muslims who wear woolen garments and practice meditation. I wish I could ask Ali Baba more about Sufis, but I'm forced to follow Master's beliefs. I don't think Ali Baba would mind my questions, but I doubt Master would take it well if he caught me asking about Sufism.

As Saja helps Mistress dress, the woman sighs. "Oh, if only I could be at their supper!" She giggles and winks at me. "I'd give my pretty little dagger to hear my husband's fortune."

I glance at Mistress as I pack up my lute. I recognize that coy voice she uses when she wants me to do something but is too ashamed to demand it. Usually it's something improper, like wanting me to spy on the neighbors. Mistress's dagger has weavelike designs carved into the hilt and a Damascus steel blade that looks like it's made of swirling water. I remember how it felt to use the paring knife to cut the ropes from Jamal's wrists. I wouldn't need to swipe an old paring knife from Cook's kitchen to have that feeling again—I'd have my own beautiful weapon. A smile creeps across my face. I decide to play along to see what she's up to this time. "But fortune-telling is evil. Besides, men and women never dine together," I say.

Mistress titters and nods as if reading my mind. "Yes, it would be unacceptable and impossible for a female to hear the fortune." She hands me the basket and winks at me again before heading out the door. "Unless she is *a slave girl, merely obeying her mistress and playing a lute behind a curtain . . .*"

I can almost feel the knife in my hand already. It's an easy trade; I'll do it.

After Mistress leaves, Saja's brow wrinkles in concern. "Be careful, Marjana. Fortune-tellers should be feared, not welcomed. And masters don't like their slaves getting involved in their affairs." She draws me close, kissing both cheeks as if I'm an old friend. Saja's hands are gentle and warm from her work.

I'm used to Jamal's rough contact and nearness, but no one's ever embraced me like a friend the way Saja does. My armor's melting like wax. I don't like that feeling. I pull away the slightest bit. "Don't worry. I can take care of myself."

7

After the muezzin's call for sunset prayers, I help Jamal spread a round embroidered cloth in the middle of the floor and arrange silver dishes over it.

"Jamal," I tell him, "Mistress's bath attendant, Saja, has a brother named Badi who may come over after his work is done." I place the gillyflowers in a vase and glance at my brother. "I thought you might become friends."

Jamal frowns and rolls his eyes.

"Saja's worried about Badi. He's joined a gang of street warriors—"

"Street warriors!" His face lights up. "Cook tells me

all about them. She says they make shop owners pay for protection against the other gangs. They get to wear helmets and fight! I wish we had one in this neighborhood."

I grab him by the ear and pull him close. "Shh! Don't let Master hear you say such things—he'll beat you."

"He never beats me."

I don't want to tell Jamal how Master was true to his word and gives Jamal's beatings to me instead. "Well, he just might if he hears such talk."

Jamal snorts. "If there were street warriors in this neighborhood, I would join them and make Master pay me to keep his shop safe. If he had done that before, I bet the Forty Thieves never would have dared taking us."

I sigh. Things aren't going as I'd planned. Irritated, I shove Jamal toward the door. "Go change, you little donkey. It's almost time to serve dinner."

We expect Master's guest any moment, and suddenly I feel a great apprehension. If fortune-tellers learn the fates of mortals from harmful jinn, Saja's right—they should be avoided, not welcomed into the home. I'm nervous about spying, too. If Master catches me, I'll get a beating instead of a pretty dagger. I place an arrangement of pistachios, dates, and pomegranates in the center of the cloth and walk to the window. Trying to calm my nerves, I gaze at the swaying fig tree outside and breathe in the smell of jasmine on the breeze.

A noise like the parade of clopping hoofs and the jangle of tambourines makes me jump. Master's brother, Ali Baba, hurries up the street, his face bright. His donkeys trot after him, their heavy baskets making a clinking sound.

A knock on the door pushes all thoughts of Ali Baba from my mind. I duck my head back inside the window. "Jamal!" I cry as I pluck up my lute. "Answer the door!" I fly across the room and slip behind the curtains Mistress and I set up in front of a doorway. I want Mistress's dagger as much as Mistress wants to know her husband's fortune.

Spreading a small carpet on the tile, I settle myself cross-legged on the floor with my lute in my lap and peer through a slight gap in the curtains. Abu-Zayed enters the room with Master. The fortune-teller is a small, stooped man with a plain face and keen eyes. He looks harmless enough. He even reminds me of someone I've seen before, but can't think of who it might be. The two men make themselves comfortable on the cushions while Jamal brings them the silver washing basin and pitcher.

I play softly while the men begin eating.

After they finish, Jamal clears the dishes and brings the coffee. I quietly set aside my lute, hoping Master will assume I've left my closet. If he suspects my presence during the fortune-telling, he won't hesitate to pull me out and beat me in front of the man.

"Come, come, my friend!" Master's deep voice is eager. "We're alone now, and I'm ready to hear my fortune! I can tell that you have it on the tip of your tongue. Please, have some coffee."

The little man raises his hand to decline the drink. "It's as you say. I've learned your fate and will waste no time in revealing it to you faithfully. Indeed, if I had the payment, you would have your fortune already."

Master shoves a bag of coins into the man's hands. "Done! Now, what have you heard from the jinn regarding my fate? I was spared being murdered by the Forty Thieves, and most of my wealth was secure in my shop when they attacked. I've married well, and my business is booming—what's next? Will my wife conceive a son, an heir? Will I become wealthier still?" He strokes his double chin in anticipation.

I don't trust the shrewd look on the fortune-teller's face. I lean forward to hear the reply.

Abu-Zayed tucks the coins into his sash and sighs heavily. "Alas, you will die childless and threadbare."

Master's cup crashes to the floor.

I jump, swallowing back the cry of surprise that rises in my throat.

The fortune-teller continues. "In the end, any dignity you have left, you will owe to the charity of your brother."

"What? My *brother*!" Master looks as if he's choked on a chicken bone. "He's a good-for-nothing Sufi! He's a poor, miserable woodcutter. I am twice the man Ali Baba is!"

Abu-Zayed glances at Master's large belly. "Be that as it may—in the end, you will be but a quarter of the man he is."

"Nonsense!" Master cries.

The old man lifts his chin in disdain. A jagged but faded scar runs across his lower neck. "On my honor, it is the truth I received from the jinn, which I faithfully revealed."

For just a moment, the fortune-teller's calm gaze rests on the gap in my curtain. His eyes narrow, and a thin smirk spreads across his face. I gasp and draw back, almost knocking against my lute.

Master struggles to his feet. "Leave my house immediately!" He swears at the man, his face growing red. "You falsifier!" With a flurry of rebukes, Master ushers him from the room. The door slams behind them.

I stare at the puddle of coffee on the floor, stunned. What should I do? Mistress is waiting for me and won't like to hear what I have to tell her. I could lie. After all, the fortune-teller is not to be trusted—maybe he *is* a falsifier. If I tell Mistress everything he said, the woman will be so upset, the whole household will suffer. But Mistress can always tell when I am lying. I sigh. If I want that knife, I have to tell Mistress what really happened.

By the time I relate the fortune and leave Mistress's chamber, I'm exhausted from the woman's wailing. But at least I have the silver dagger, which makes me feel the way I did that day I escaped the Forty Thieves— stronger, in control. I walk along the corridor of the harem to the tiny room Jamal and I share and see Saja standing outside the carved wooden screen, smiling and squinting through the cut design. "I brought Badi," she says.

So the girl braved the evil bathhouse mistress and came after all. I use my new knife on the shutter screen's lock and almost have the catch pried free when Saja cries, "Stop, Marjana—you'll break it! Your master will be furious. I shouldn't stay long, anyway. I have to finish my work." She glances nervously behind her. "But Badi is done with his."

I peer down at Saja's brother. He looks Jamal's age. Drops of water from the fountain spray speckle his white tunic, and his knees are scratched up. I wave him toward the back of the house. "Jamal is digging in the garden."

Badi nods and runs off.

Saja leans closer and holds on to the screen, trying to see me better. The breeze carries the scent of lavender from her hair.

She whispers, "Marjana, after you left, I kept thinking of the song you played on your lute. The words wouldn't leave my mind."

"But there were no words, only music."

"Well, maybe no one else could hear the words, but I did. They were about wanting things like freedom. And someone to care."

I look away. Saja had somehow broken open the lock on my heart.

"The song said exactly what I was feeling. You have a

gift, Marjana. Your music reveals the listener's secrets to themselves."

I don't know what to say. Badi's and Jamal's laughter drift to us from the garden. "It's just a simple song." I shrug, feeling uncomfortable.

Saja smiles. "I should leave now—I'm supposed to be doing laundry. If the mistress of the baths finds out I've been gone, she'll wring *me* out and hang me up to dry! Here, this is for you." She takes something from her sash.

"But I don't have anything to trade—"

"No, it's a gift." Saja slips her fingers through the screen and drops something small into my palm before hurrying away.

I lift my hand to the light streaming through the screen, curious to see Saja's gift. A whole cardamom. What was it Leila said the cardamom from her soul sister meant?

You are my secret-keeper.

The same warmth that flooded over me at Saja's

embrace comes rushing back. I never had a friend before. I squeeze the green cardamom in my fist. But friendship means trust. I don't know if I want to share my secrets with Saja the way she shares things with me. The thought scares me.

"Marjana!" Mistress cries. "I need my smelling salts! Oh, I'm so distressed."

I breathe in the fresh scent of the smooth seed pod. As I run to soothe Mistress's worries about her husband's fortune, I pop the cardamom in my mouth. The cool flavor bursts on my tongue when I chew, bringing to mind the refreshing peppermint oil at the bathhouse. Something inside me longs to trust Saja. But I know better than to believe in that safe, loving feeling I lost when Mother died. I know how easily such a feeling can be pulled out from under me, leaving me feeling empty and alone.

When I reach Mistress's chamber, I spit the seed pod into my hand and let it fall to the floor.

8

Early the next morning, I wake to the sound of brisk knocking. Throwing on a cloak, I run to the front door and squint into the light. Ali Baba's wife, Leila, stands there, beaming like the sun.

"As-salaam alaykum, dear. I'm so sorry to call this early, but I'm in desperate need of a measure. Would you ask my sister-in-law if I might borrow hers?"

The woman seems so cheerful. The combined brightness of the morning and Leila's smile makes my head ache. I'm still reeling from the previous night and the drama I endured when Mistress learned her husband's fortune. I force a smile for Leila and run to Mistress's dressing room to relay the request.

"Has the woman gone mad?" Mistress scowls. "What on earth could she have such a great quantity of that she needs a measure—their family is poor as the dirt! And at this hour!"

"Perhaps they've had some good fortune. Shall I fetch it for her?"

At the word "fortune," the color drains from Mistress's face. She hesitates, no doubt recalling Abu-Zayed's prediction. Mistress bites her lip, thinking. "This is what we shall do. Tell her I need to wash the measure, first, and then I'll send you over with it directly. In the meantime, I'll spread a little cooking fat underneath, on the bottom of the measure." Her eyes light up. "A grain of millet, rye, or whatever it is she's measuring will stick to the fat, and the mystery shall be solved!"

"Of course." I smile as I go tell Leila I'll be over with it shortly. While I wait for Mistress to prepare the measure to her liking, I return to the small room I share with Jamal. He's still asleep on his mat.

"Get up, you lazy little donkey." I poke his shoulder with my toe. "What did you and Badi do last night?" I'd been busy consoling Mistress and had fallen asleep before Jamal came to bed.

He rolls over and groans. A dark bruise covers his left eye.

"What is this?" I grab his shoulders and stare at his face "Did Badi hit you? Your eye is black and blue! That brat! When I get my hands on him—"

Jamal shoots up from the floor, a grin spreading across his face. "It's blue? Really?"

"Why did he do this to you?"

Jamal brushes my hand away from his face. "It doesn't hurt. And Badi didn't do it. We're friends!"

Although I'd wanted Saja's brother to become friends with Jamal, now I'm not so sure. "But if Badi didn't hit you, then who—"

"Marjana!" Mistress calls from the other room in an impatient voice.

I roll my eyes and head for the door. "You will tell

me *everything* you and Badi did, little donkey, as soon as I come back."

Mistress, beaming with pride at the plan she concocted, hands me the prepared measure, a large cup for scooping and measuring grain; I can't even see the layer of fat coating the bottom. As she gives me directions to Ali Baba's house, I think how sneaky Mistress is! First the scheme to eavesdrop on the fortune-teller and now this. Her idea was amusing at first, but now it seems trivial. What did the boys do last night? A sinking feeling comes over me. I slip the measure under my arm and leave the house. Saja had been so happy when I suggested that Badi become friends with Jamal. I should have paid more attention, kept an eye on them. I can't shake the nervous clenching in my stomach.

It's only a short distance to Ali Baba's house. The family lives on a small, nearby alleyway. The road and dwelling are ancient and need repair. Ali Baba didn't inherit as much money or marry a wealthy man's daughter as his brother had, and his poverty is obvious.

I knock on the faded wooden door. After several moments of waiting, I try again. They probably have no servants to receive guests, so I let myself in. Before I can call out, voices reach me from a back room, and I start in that direction. A burst of merry laughter makes me pause.

"*Sesame!* Can you believe it, wife?"

More laughter pours from the room, accompanied by the clinking noise of a tambourine, just as I had heard the night before.

"And to think *sesame* will change lives!"

So, that's what they want to measure—sesame seeds. I open my mouth to call out a greeting, when someone speaks from behind me.

"As-salaam alaykum."

I jump. Rasheed, Ali Baba's son, reclines like a sultan on a bed of ragged cushions in the corner of the room. He laughs at my surprise.

My face grows hot as a brick oven. "Why didn't you come to the door and let me in?" I snap, forgetting for a moment that he's Master's nephew. I bite my tongue, wondering if he'll leap up to strike me.

Rasheed's grin fades. He turns away, but doesn't get up.

I could kick myself for my foolishness. Lazy Rasheed will tell his uncle, and I'll be punished. "I thought—" I stop. Why should I explain? It will only make him feel smug. I approach the young man and hand him the measure. "Here. Your mother needs to borrow this from my mistress." I want to ask why he doesn't help his father cut wood, but I have no intention of starting a conversation with him.

I glance at his face. His eyes are dark and deep. They tell me nothing. Feeling exposed, I instinctively touch my headscarf. I want to turn and leave without a word, shaming him with rude silence, but Master won't hesitate to try and slap the fire out of me if his nephew complains about my behavior.

I bow stiffly. "As-salaam alaykum," I mumble before hurrying from the house. I fly down the old road, stumbling over ruts and stones, cursing under my breath.

I storm through the harem door. "Now tell me what trouble you and Badi got into last night!" I yell, taking my frustration out on my brother.

Jamal is wrapping his turban around his head. I yank him by the ear and the ring of cloth on his forehead slips down about his neck like an ox yoke.

"Ow!" he cries, and bats at me.

I let go, and he stomps on my foot. I resist the urge to scream or hit him, and cross my arms over my chest instead. "What did you and Badi *do*?"

Jamal flings his turban at me. "Something brave and exciting. We're doing it again tonight, and you can't stop me. You're not my father or my master. You're just a slave."

"So are you!"

"But you're a *girl* slave; you're nothing. I'm a war—"

Cook's sour voice rings through the house. "Jamal, you louse, get off your mat and come peel the pears!"

He grabs his head cloth, sticks out his tongue, and dashes away.

Why is he being such a stupid little donkey? Steaming, I bend down, roll up his mat, and throw the rug as hard as I can at the window screen. It hits the lock I pried loose the night before and knocks the shutter screens open. The rug flies right out the window like a magic carpet.

"Aiyeee!" cries a voice from outside.

I rush to the sill.

Saja sits on a squashed rosebush, a bewildered look on her face. She rubs her head. "Is that how you air out your rugs? It's very dangerous."

"Saja, what are you doing here?"

She stands up and puts her hands on her hips, pretending to be angry. "That's all you have to say? *Saja, what are you doing here? How about I'm sorry, Saja, for trying to kill you with a rug—please reveal the important matter you must have come here to tell me.*"

I can't keep a laugh from escaping. "I'm sorry! I didn't mean to hurt you."

Saja leans over the window ledge. "I have to hurry. I snuck away from the bathhouse, but I'll be missed soon.

I'm so afraid of getting caught." She hesitates and bites her lip. "I came to tell you I saw Jamal for a moment last night. Badi brought him to the slave quarters at the baths. I'm pretty sure he took him to the street warriors, but of course, I couldn't follow them on my own—it was almost dark. I know you said it's just a game, but sometimes I see warriors through the window, fighting in the streets and breaking into shops. I'm so worried. Badi's all I've got."

I swallow hard. "Saja, I—"

"Badi says he's coming for Jamal again, tonight. I just thought you would want to know. I need to get back to the bathhouse." Saja squeezes my hand and lets go, leaving a smooth stick of cinnamon in her palm.

A soul sisters' gift. Leila said it means *I trust you.*

Saja's trust creates a heaviness in my stomach and a lightness in my head at the same time, as if I've drawn a long pull of smoke from a hookah. "Wait!" I catch her sleeve.

Saja turns, waiting.

I breathe in the warm scent of the cinnamon stick. "Thank you." I'm not used to saying the words. They feel foreign on my lips, difficult to get out right. Making sure I'm still alone in the room, I lower my voice. "I know the street battles aren't a game—Jamal came home with a black eye. We can't sit by and watch our brothers grow up to become thieves and murderers like the Forty Thieves." The devil-man's green serpent slithers across my thoughts. I take a deep breath. "The Forty Thieves killed Master's guards and stole most of the people who once lived in this house. They stole Jamal and me, too, but we were lucky to escape."

Saja's eyes widen. "May Allah protect us!" she whispers.

"Badi and Jamal might be more vinegar than honey, but they are our brothers, and I swear an oath I'll find a way to stop them before they become common thieves, or . . . worse. First, I want to see these gangs myself. Tonight."

"But we can't follow them. You know girls don't go out at night. It's too dangerous, even for slave girls."

I glance over my shoulder. My heart is a big fist, beating down a door. I stare hard at Saja and whisper, "Then we shall not be girls."

CHAPTER

9

I sit on my mat, strumming softly on my lute. I've finished my work for the evening and I am practicing a new song. Using the melody of my earlier song, I create a new piece from it, adding fluttering, rising notes, like the wings of birds soaring into the sky. I'll teach Jamal the beat to go with it—the rhythm of a heart thumping ever faster.

Jamal's singing drifts through the open yard as he brings lamp oil into the kitchen from the storehouse. My fingers fumble over the strings, clashing the notes together. I breathe in deeply, trying to calm my nerves as I wait for Saja. The light's fading fast. We won't have much time to change clothes before Badi comes to fetch Jamal.

As if my thoughts have summoned her, Saja's wide eyes appear at the window. She opens the shutter screens and drops a basket over the sill. "Help me up!" she whispers. "Hurry, before someone sees me!"

I help her over the ledge and wait for her to catch her breath. Saja's cheeks are the color of roses, and her hair's come loose in soft wispy curls on her forehead. She digs into her basket.

"This is for you." Saja hands me a tiny soapstone vial. "Essence of jasmine. It's not much, but it's very potent, so you only need to use a little at a time."

I don't know what to say. "But you don't owe me this." I lift the vial to my nose and breathe in the strong sweet scent.

Saja puts her hands on her hips. "You are the hardest person to give a gift to that I ever saw. Don't you like it?

"Yes, jasmine reminds me of my mother. It was her favorite flower."

"I'm glad you have it to remember her by." Saja smiles.

"Look, I brought these." She draws two long pieces of linen from her basket. "To bind us down on top and make us flat as pan bread."

I laugh and raise an eyebrow. Saja's my age, but even under a loose garment, her shapely figure is obvious. "The binding cloths will work for me, but I think it will take something a little more . . . powerful . . . to change you into pan bread!"

Her face turns the color of a red apple.

"I know just the thing." I run out of the room and come back with a large leather waist girdle with fastening strings. "Mistress sometimes wears this. If it's strong enough to flatten her middle, then it's strong enough to flatten your top."

Saja takes off her qamis and sirwal and slips the girdle around her chest. I pull the strings together in the back for her.

"Ow! I can't breathe," she cries. "I'd prefer not to die in order to become a boy. If you tighten it any more, I'll pass out!"

I tie the strings in place. "All right. But you still look . . . lumpy."

Saja rolls her eyes. "It will be dark. No one will notice." She twirls the long strip of linen in the air and smirks. "Ha! Now it's your turn, little pan-bread boy!"

I wriggle out of my qamis and sirwal and lift my arms as Saja wraps the linen around my upper body. Like a dance, I twirl in the opposite direction as Saja winds the linen, until we come to the end of it. Her laugh is a bubbling pool; it makes me want to jump right in.

"Absolutely non-lumpy," Saja declares as she secures the cloth and sits down on my mat.

Only one thing left. I slide a ribbon through the sheath of the silver knife that Mistress gave me and tie the ribbon around my thigh. I've slipped a sprig of jasmine into the hidden compartment in its hilt.

The color drains from Saja's face. "You're taking a *weapon*?" She reaches out and runs a finger over the design on the silver handle. "Aren't you afraid to use it?"

"I might need it." I hesitate, wondering how much I should say about how I feel. Saja has shared so much with me that it gives me the courage to open up to her, too. I take a deep breath and go on. "Saja, in your dream about the perfume shop, you are your own mistress; you're free. I wish I were free, too. Having a knife makes me feel that I am. It reminds me of how I felt when I cut the ropes around my wrists and Jamal's and escaped the Forty Thieves.

"I've never met anyone like you." Saja stands. "What makes you so brave?"

I don't know what to say. I don't feel brave. I can barely talk about my own feelings without trembling. How can I be brave if the simple idea of trusting someone scares me more than anything else? I shrug, not knowing how to answer.

"Well, I wish I could be that way." She sighs.

Saja's not a fool, but she makes herself vulnerable— giving gifts, sharing secrets and dreams, not knowing for sure how she'll be treated in return. If it isn't foolishness, it must be some kind of courage that I don't have. "You're braver than you know."

Saja looks surprised. "How—"

Someone runs past the outside window.

"That's Badi coming for Jamal," I whisper.

Saja nods, her breath coming fast. "We should hurry. We have to be ready to follow them when they leave." She digs through her basket and tosses a wad of clothing to me. "When I did laundry, I smuggled these—the attendants wear them in the men's bathhouse."

I struggle into the long qamis. The cut of the garments is trimmer than I'm used to. I grab my scarf off the floor and start wrapping it around my hair as Saja puts on her own headdress. When we look at each other in boys' clothes and girls' headdresses, we burst out laughing.

But I cringe inside at the thought of leaving behind my headscarf. My thoughts usually flow freely onto my features, safely hidden behind the scarf if I choose to become invisible. Now I have to leave it behind.

Saja's grin falters. "I don't know, Marjana. If we're dis-covered, we could be beaten . . . or worse."

I squirm under the uncomfortable clothing. I force my voice to sound light. "No one will give us a second glance. It will be dark, like you said." I rummage through the basket and pull out the turban cloths. We pin up our hair and wind the material around our heads as quickly as we can. When we finish, we stare at each other.

Saja giggles. "We're boys." Her voice sounds tiny, like a small child's.

"Warriors," I correct her. I clear my throat and speak in a deep voice. "And we must talk like this." I swagger to the window. "And walk this way."

Saja laughs.

"And say tough things to each other like 'Get out of my way, you crusty piece of camel dung, or I'll knock you in the—'"

"Oh, hurry!" Saja squeaks. "I hear Badi outside!"

My heart beats in double time as Saja and I crouch near

the window and watch our younger brothers pass.

"Let's go, Marjana, or we'll lose them!"

Before we slip over the ledge into the falling dark, I grab Saja by the elbow. "Wait!"

Her eyes grow round as melons. "What's wrong?"

I try to smile as I whisper, "Whatever you do tonight, Lumpy, *don't call me Marjana*!"

10

Saja and I hurry after our brothers through the darkening streets of Baghdad. A purple streak lingers on the edge of the horizon, giving the streets a strange, smoky hue. The moon hangs like a great silver bowl in the sky. Snatches of light flicker from windows.

I've never seen Baghdad after sunset prayers, when all proper females are safely tucked away in their homes for the night. My skin tingles with excitement.

As Badi and Jamal near the bathhouse, they're joined by a group of older boys wearing white qamis like the ones we are wearing. They're just young slaves like us, not warriors. But there's an eagerness in their faces and a boldness in their steps that make them look less like slaves and more like soldiers. Even little Jamal carries himself differently. He holds his shoulders straight and his head high; he looks taller.

We keep a safe distance from them. I want to see what our brothers are up to and protect them, but if the boys get a good look at our faces, all will be over. We slink around corners and linger in the shadows, trying to stay far enough behind to escape notice. When the boys pass through the empty marketplace and turn down an unfamiliar alley, I nudge Saja's arm.

"Hurry!"

We race through the eerie, deserted market square. It looks lonely and naked in the moonlight. I trip over something huddled in my path. It's the old storyteller who I saw a few days ago in the square. Now he's sleeping against a stall. His small frame and ragged clothing had pulled at my heart that morning. By day, the homeless man recites ancient tales for a coin. I whisper in his ear, "As-salaam alaykum, sir. Forgive me."

The little man smells of cheap wine and dirty linen. His eyes remain shut, but he replies, "Wa alaykum as-salaam. 'Tis nothing, grand lady. Don't you mind about me." One runny eye pops open, and I jump. When he sees my turban and boy clothes, the storyteller's eye narrows. "Ah! 'Tis a story there. I will dream on it. Looks like the jinn are busy tonight." With that, his eye slides shut and he curls back into a ball and begins to snore.

"Hurry, Marjana; we're going to lose them!" Saja cries.

But I don't hurry. My eyes fix on the storyteller, all the warmth draining from my face. "Saja, if I'd made such a stupid mistake in front of anyone else, we'd be exposed. We have to remember to talk like boys. And we have to think of names—you can't keep calling me Marjana."

"Marjana, come *on!*" Saja cries, too nervous to pay attention. She grabs my hand and pulls me across the square toward the dark alleyway where the boys disappeared. Something skitters across our path. Saja shrieks.

"A rat," I whisper, my heart fluttering. "It's only a rat." Except for the rodent, the alley appears empty.

"Now what do we do?"

"Let's keep going. They're probably not far ahead."

We hurry to the end of the alley, which opens onto a larger road with several side streets intersecting it. A flash of running figures catches my eye, and I race down the street with Saja after the group of boys who have just turned the corner near the mosque.

I push my long legs to run faster. The night air on my face wakes up my heart, my limbs. The slap of the knife against my thigh urges me on. Saja gasps for breath behind me, but I can't stop. I don't want the exhilarating feeling to go away. I need to run. I barrel around the bend in the road, but the boys are lingering against the wall, around the corner, talking. When I skid to a stop right in front of them, Saja comes crashing into me from behind, and we fall in a heap at their feet.

For an instant, the boys are caught off guard. Their eyes grow wide, and their mouths drop open as we get up and brush ourselves off. In that moment, I search their faces and realize that Badi and Jamal aren't among them. This is a different group of boys. I hook Saja's arm and turn to go in the opposite direction.

By now, the boys recover from their surprise.

"Hey, you!" one of them shouts. "This is our street. What gang do you fight with?"

I make my voice sound deep. "We're just looking for our brothers." I keep walking with Saja, not daring to turn around.

"You aren't in a gang? Looks like you're from the bath-house. Come here!" The voice has something of a threat in it, and I hesitate, my heart pounding in my ears. Saja's arm goes limp beside me. I make up my mind and turn around to face him.

He's a tall, wiry boy with ragged clothes and a chipped tooth. If he wasn't so disheveled, he might almost be handsome, but he doesn't wear a turban, and his curly hair looks like a bird's nest, with bits of leaves woven in. He saunters over to us. I cringe as he squints at my eyes. I long for my scarf.

"You're bathies." He isn't asking, so much as telling us.

I nod. "We're from the bathhouse. But we're new there. We don't know anything about gangs."

The boy's eyebrows rise, and his face eases into a grin. "Well, you've come to the right place. We'll teach you all about it. You can be in our gang—we're better than the bathies. There's a big meeting tonight with all the gangs together, so we could use you. Red Beard will be there, too; he's leader of all the gangs."

My mind races. If all the gangs are meeting together and we stay with this group, we can find the bathies. That's the gang Badi and Jamal will be in.

The boy chews on something tucked between his lower lip and his teeth. He turns to spit, and the black mess lands near Saja's toe. She screws up her face, but doesn't say a word, much to my relief.

"Everybody calls me Stinger," he says. "Because of this." He shoves his fist toward my face, stopping just inches from my chin.

I wince.

He's mounted a wildcat's fang on a ring around his

middle finger. It points directly at my nose. I swallow.

"What are your names?" Stinger demands.

I gesture toward Saja, trying not to look at the ring. "He's, umm . . . he's . . ." I grasp at the first word that pops into my head. "Lumpy. Everybody calls him that. Because . . . that's . . . what he is."

The boy nods a greeting at Saja, who blushes and reaches for a curl to wind around her finger, forgetting she wears a turban.

I almost kick her.

Stinger doesn't seem to notice Saja's mistake and asks her, "So, what does everybody call him?" He jerks his head in my direction.

Saja glances at me. "They call him Khubz," she says in her best boy voice. It sounds like she's swallowed a peach pit.

At Saja's words, I almost choke, trying to suppress a nervous laugh. Khubz is the name for flat pan bread.

Stinger cracks another grin, and I would swear Saja's blushing again. It looks as if she might even let out a giggle. If she does, it will all be over. Fortunately, Stinger doesn't seem to notice her reactions.

"We're on our way to the dumping grounds." He slips a mallet from his belt and twirls it in his fingers. "I hope you boys brought weapons."

11

Saja and I follow Stinger and his gang through Baghdad's labyrinth of streets and alleyways. The group is made up of about a dozen homeless boys, all skinny, ratty-haired creatures. I feel sorry for them—it isn't easy scrounging for food on the streets and fighting for what clothing can be found. But I also envy them. They're their own masters. They go wherever they want, whenever they feel like it. They belong to themselves. I can see why their way of life is so enticing to Jamal.

The gang turns onto a steep, uphill road lined with jasmine into one of the wealthier neighborhoods. Stinger slows down, and the boys walk reverently over the jutting cobbled stones, gazing at the beautiful houses they pass. Some of the boys even peek through the cracks in the wooden shutters. The breezes sweep over the hill and pick up the heavy sweet scent of jasmine.

As we go, the pretty streets gradually turn into shoddy lanes, full of rough spots and holes. Before long, dilapidated huts replace the fine houses lining the street. The smell of jasmine floating on the breeze turns to putrid garbage. It's as if one world's melting into another. Soon we reach the dumping grounds. Saja pinches her nose at the stench of the rubble.

Stinger pauses on the edge of the grounds, scoping out the land. Other gangs stream down the slope into the maze of trash heaps, heading to the center, where a small fire burns. There, a group of boys in brilliant white qamis stand out like a string of pearls in a pile of dung. The bathhouse boys. *Is Jamal in the group?*

"There he is!" Stinger points, and for a moment, I think he's reading my mind. Stinger's face is aglow. He grins so wide, the cracks on his lips start to bleed a little. He points at a large horse, ridden by a tall, thin man with darkened eyes and high cheekbones. His long beard is a striking red, and his flowing clothes and turban a garish orange. The leader of the child street gangs. Perched on the man's saddle in front of him rides a young boy wearing a woven helmet.

Saja leans in close. "I see Badi—he looks all right—but what on earth is Jamal doing up there?" Saja's voice quivers and her breath tickles my ear.

A coldness shivers through my bones as I watch Saja's brother gazing up at the rider and the boy. I squint at the two figures on the horse and nearly cry out as if I've been pricked by a scorpion when I recognize the boy's crooked grin. Jamal. "That little donkey!" I whisper.

Stinger shakes his head, still staring at the leader. "Looks like Red Beard picked himself another lamb from the fold to be his little pet." He laughs and nudges his friends. "We'll see how long this one lasts."

What could that mean? My heart beats like a fist against my ribs. "Why, what's going to happen to him?" I struggle to keep my voice calm.

"Oh, everybody wants to ride with Red Beard. It means he thinks you might ride in his place one day. When he picks somebody, the boys have to see if he's worthy, so we rough up the kid later to find out what he's really made of."

My body tenses. "But he's so little—this is mad!"

"I know." Stinger nods. "This one doesn't stand a chance. Red Beard should choose someone stronger who can do the job properly." He puffs out his chest. "Someone older—a gang leader that knows something about real fighting!"

I glance at Saja, who heard the whole thing. She clears her throat and asks, "So what's going to happen tonight? What's the big meeting about?"

Stinger's face lights up. "Red Beard tells us which gangs are going to fight against each other tonight and which ones will break into the shops."

"He *tells* you to fight each other?" I interrupt.

"That's how the games are played."

"Games?" Saja cries. "You call fighting each other with weapons and stealing from shops a *game*?"

"Aw, we don't get to keep the stuff—Red Beard's men round it up and report who did the best fighting. That gang wins, and those boys get to go to Red Beard's camp with his men and celebrate with feasting like you've never seen! You should hear the grand stories the boys tell of the delicious food that seems to appear from out of nowhere. No one knows how it's done, but everyone wants to go see for themselves! The men say one day the best boys will get to join them and keep the stuff they steal. Sometimes Red Beard even chooses one of the older boys to replace one of his men when he loses one."

Saja and I exchange worried looks.

"But that's not the tail end of it." Stinger laughs and twirls his mallet in the air. "There's talk about a secret bigger than you could ever dream of. And if you end up riding with Red Beard for good, he'll let you in on it." He catches the mallet and shoves it back into his belt. "And I aim to be one of the few who finds out."

Stinger gallops down the hill to join the crowd of boys in the center. I follow Saja and the rest of the gang after him. Everyone wants to get next to the man on the horse. The boys jostle each other as the crowd presses in. I feel sick with so many strangers this close. Their faces loom too near; their hands and elbows push into my arms, my back. I hold my breath and screw my eyes shut.

Red Beard's voice rises above the din of the mob, and everyone quiets down. "I've called you here today on a small business matter." The flames cast flickering light and shadows over his features and blackened eyes, making it difficult to see his face and giving him a ghoulish look. "It appears the wealthy merchant, Jaffar, who lives on Umar Hill, has gone on a journey. Fortunately, he paid the bathhouse gang to protect his property before he left. When he returns, he shall hear how valiantly they fought for him. Of course, it is a shame he will also discover his property looted despite their greatest efforts."

The boys chuckle and nudge each other with their elbows. I try to look at Jamal without him seeing me. He sits straight and tall in front of the man, his face beaming as if he's just found Cook's secret store of sweets. At least he's safe—for now. I cringe to think of what Stinger and the other boys might do to him after the battle.

Red Beard takes the woven helmet from Jamal's head and throws it to one of the bathhouse boys. A small scuffle breaks out as some of his companions try to wrestle it from him, but they back down when the boy draws his "sword," a sharpened stick as long as his arm. He proudly tears off his turban and puts the helmet on.

"Take four gangs—two to fight, two to break in," Red Beard orders. He pulls out another helmet and scans Stinger's group. He turns his face toward us and seems to be looking right at me, though it's too hard to tell with the fire making shadows flicker across his eyes. A chill goes through my bones. Forgetting I'm not wearing it, I reach to touch my scarf. My fingers grasp air and graze my bare face. Red Beard freezes when he catches my careless gesture—I feel his eyes on me.

"You—bathhouse boy. What's your name?"

I shrink back, trying to find something to disappear into.

Stinger steps toward Red Beard. "That's Khubz. He and Lumpy don't even know anything. This is their first time."

The man doesn't alter his stance or turn toward Stinger, but continues to address me. "Take two gangs and fight against the others. The rest will guard the looters." He throws the helmet at me.

My hands instinctively reach out and catch it. I stand frozen like a statue, clutching the helmet in front of me. The man smiles faintly beneath his red beard. It makes my skin crawl. Does he know I'm in disguise?

"No bathie's going to lead my gang!" Stinger snatches the helmet from me and pushes me down. The fang on his ring cuts my cheek as it flies past. I swallow back a cry of pain and thrust my feet between Stinger's, forcing his legs apart. He topples to the ground, still clutching the helmet. I lunge for it. If I lead Stinger's gang, I can control them—keep them away from Badi and Jamal. But Stinger swings the flat side of his mallet at me, hitting me across the chest and knocking me backward.

Saja cries out and runs to me. "Are you all right, Marjana?" she whispers, clutching my arm. She unwinds a bit of her turban cloth and presses it to the bleeding cut.

I nod. The wind's knocked out of me and my chest aches, but I notice Red Beard still has his face turned toward me, so I brush Saja's hands away and muster up the courage to lift my face as Stinger pulls the helmet on and starts yelling orders to his gang. Out of the corner of my eye, I finally see Red Beard's head turn away. Jamal didn't recognize me, yet this stranger suspected at once that I was wearing a disguise.

After the two helmeted leaders organize their troops, they light some torches in the fire and pass them around. When all's ready, Red Beard raises his sword in the air and shouts, "To Umar Hill!"

The wild cry that rises from the gangs makes me jump. Saja squeals and seizes my arm, but no one notices us—everyone's on the move. As the group surges up the hill to the city, I try keeping Jamal and Badi in my sights. I grab Saja's sleeve so we won't get separated as the flood of bodies carries us off toward Umar Hill.

12

The bathhouse boys arrive at the merchant Jaffar's home first and position themselves in battle formation in the middle of the street. The boy wearing the helmet rides on the back of another boy like a warrior on a horse, his stick sword thrust into the air. Stinger, too, jumps onto the back of one of his friends and raises his mallet.

"Marjana!" Saja almost yanks my arm out of its socket. "What are we going to do?" she whispers. "We wanted to keep Badi and Jamal safe, not fight like them!"

But before I can answer, loud crashes erupt near the house. The looters have begun their work. The boys are breaking down the doors and windows of Jaffar's store and warehouse. As if this is a signal, the two leaders give a war cry. Their "horses" bolt forward.

The rush of gangs follows, and Saja and I are knocked over as the boys gallop toward one another, waving their weapons in the air and shouting. I help Saja to her feet and slip the knife from its sheath. Holding it out in front of me like a shield, I struggle to push my way out of the mob, dragging Saja with me.

We almost reach the safety of a low wall, when a flying rock hits Saja between the shoulder blades. She cries out and stumbles into a clump of bushes. I whip around to face our attacker, but whoever threw the rock is lost in the dark sea of battling warriors. I crawl into the cover of the bushes with Saja.

"Are you all right?"

"Yes." Saja sniffs. "But I can't see Badi anywhere. It's so dark. And crazy."

I peer out at the fight. If any citizens dare investigate the scene, they will think one rival gang is protecting the neighborhood by warding off the other. I scan the frantic movements of the bathhouse boys as they fight Stinger's gang. The flash of a small white qamis near the wall catches my eye. The boy's arm is raised, ready to throw a rock into the fray. I squint through the darkness at the figure. The torchlight plays with my vision, but I'm sure it's Saja's brother. Praise Allah!

As I head toward him, a bigger boy plows into him, knocking him backward, then lifts his club, ready to strike. A surge of energy courses through my body, and I bolt out of the bushes. I grab the older boy's club and sling it over the wall. His jaw falls open as he watches it disappear into the darkness. His mouth and eyebrows gather into a knot, and he rushes at me like a demon.

I twirl away easily and slip behind the boy in one graceful move. Club Boy turns and lunges for me again, but I duck at the last moment and spring away from him like a cat. He loses his balance. With a push, I help send him tumbling over the wall.

The boy swears at me as he picks himself up and runs off to find his club. My blood races and my arms tingle.

I'm breathless. Fighting's almost as exhilarating as dancing. When I reach out a hand to help the smaller boy to his feet, I realize he's not even Saja's brother.

Saja calls out in her girl voice, "Marjana, look out!" She barrels toward me, wielding a branch like a weapon, and runs right past me.

I spin around. Club Boy's charging straight at me, ready to strike, but Saja knocks him down before he even has the chance to swing. He falls to the ground, moaning and rubbing his head.

I gasp. "Saja! He could have killed me with that club. You saved me—"

"There's Badi!" She points through the crowd. I can't see him.

At that moment, a great shout rises up. I turn to find the bathhouse gang running away and Stinger's boys rejoicing. They throw their weapons in the air and make loud cheering noises. The looters have finished their job, and several men on horseback arrive with Red Beard. My brother still perches on the man's saddle like a miniature captain, his face glowing with importance. All the boys gather around the horses. I need to get to Jamal before Stinger does. I run to join the group.

"Nice work out there, Khubz." Stinger appears beside me. "I saw how you dodged that big oaf and knocked him over the wall." He slaps me on the back and grins. "Too bad he was one of ours." He laughs. "Doesn't matter—we won." He eyes my dagger. "Nice knife."

"Now what happens?" I ask as the last of the gang members join the group.

"We go to Red Beard's camp to celebrate!" Stinger gazes up at the leader. His smile quickly fades as he looks at Jamal. "And we'll make lamb stew out of Red Beard's little pet. He won't recognize the kid by the time I get through with him."

A small figure in a white tunic lunges toward Stinger's gang crying out, "No! Leave him alone." It's Badi, punching his way into the group of older boys.

One of them laughs and shoves Badi into the wall, knocking off his turban. The clunking sound of his head hitting stone makes me feel ill. Saja bolts over to Badi, who lies on the ground like a crumpled dishrag. She glances up at me, her eyes pleading for me to help.

But I can't move, afraid of what might happen to Jamal. Stinger still glares at him sitting on Red Beard's horse. He points and yells, "Hey, you little turd—your bathies lost, and you didn't even fight in this battle." He scratches his chin with the fang on his ring so Jamal can see it. "Come on down here and show us what kind of warrior you really are!"

I grab Stinger's arm. "No!"

He almost drops his mallet in surprise.

I try making my voice sound rough. "He's mine. You stole my helmet—this time it's my turn." I shove Stinger aside; he stumbles back against his mates. "I'll make sure he never rides with Red Beard again," I say.

Stinger stands there gawking as I push my way through the crowd. He starts laughing behind me. "Flatten him like pan bread, Khubz!"

If I stop moving forward, I'll never do what has to

be done. The wind of fate whips at my back, pushing me on. I tighten my fingers around my dagger and walk up to Red Beard's horse. Avoiding eye contact with Jamal, I stare at the leader's beard.

I feel the man's gaze and flinch, but don't turn away. "Let the boy down." I mean to say it forcefully, but it comes out too softly.

Red Beard shoves me away with his foot as I were a bothersome puppy. But I won't leave without my brother. I swallow my fear and raise my dagger. "Give me the boy!"

The man's fingers clamp on to my wrist. I gasp. *What will he do to me?* He takes me off balance and pulls, lifting and swinging me up onto the horse between himself and Jamal. My brother's small familiar frame is finally within reach. But now we're both trapped.

As Red Beard slaps his horse's reins, I catch a glimpse of Saja cradling Badi in her arms. And then the horse shoots forward, galloping toward the woods at the edge of the dumping grounds, with Stinger's gang running and cheering behind them.

13

At the edge of the woods, sparks from the men's bonfire ricochet off golden plates and silver goblets. A banquet. for half a hundred people. Roasted hens, melons, figs, and cheese. Cakes and goblets of sparkling juice. The boys are stunned at their good fortune and everyone's jostling for a place around the fire. But I can't eat a thing. I have to get Jamal out of here.

I pull him close to me and cup my hand around his ear to tell him what Stinger and his boys will do to him at any moment, but he pushes me away and reaches for a cake.

Red Beard stands so near, watching us. The fire's to

his back and his face is in darkness.

Stinger's ignoring the feast and heads straight for Jamal.

"Jamal!" I try to warn him.

Before I can stop him, Stinger shoves Jamal to the ground.

I reach for my knife, but Red Beard's fingers grasp the hilt before mine.

He slides my knife from the sheath and over my thigh, drawing a slender line of red across my skin.

I gasp in pain and shock.

Red Beard laughs. He holds the knife in both hands as if he's going to break it in half over his knee, but I grab it from him.

The boys circle around Jamal like a pack of wolves.

I have to do something.

Now.

My hand shaking, I pull a burning log from the fire and throw the fiery stick into the nearby woods.

Immediately, the flames devour the dry forest leaves

and frighten the mules loaded with loot so that they bolt in every direction. The wind whisks up the flames and carries them along.

Red Beard's men rush to gather the mules and put out the growing forest fire, and I pull Jamal from Stinger's grasp as the boys hurry to help the men.

"You're coming with me, you little donkey."

Jamal's eyes grow round as kettledrums, and the light of recognition dawns on his face. I grab him by the ear and drag him away as everyone shouts and runs toward the fire. Smoke fills the air, stinging our eyes. My hand burns from the hot log, and my heart races like a galloping horse as the flames whip into the night.

Bursting from the woods, free from the gang and Red Beard, I want to shout or sing or dance. I saved my brother and got us safely away.

But Jamal's not grateful. He pinches my arm and kicks at my ankles all the way to Umar Hill. "Let me go! I want to go back—Red Beard won't let me ride with him again if he thinks I ran away instead of helping put out the fire."

I glance around, looking for Saja and Badi. "Jamal, those boys were going to hurt you. Even Badi knew that— didn't you see how he tried to fight them off?" Saja, too, had rushed to my rescue and saved me from Club Boy. The brave proof of Saja's friendship makes my heart swell. Should I have stayed to help her with Badi? The last time I saw her, Saja was crying and holding her brother in her arms.

A column of gray smoke rises from the forest behind us as we hurry up the hill. Jaffar's neighbors have come to investigate the warriors' damage. Men's voices call to one another in the street. I keep to the wall, out of sight. A quivering feeling of unease tightens in my chest. Where did Badi and Saja go?

On the ground near a bush, a large dark stain is visible among the shadows and patches of silver-blue moonlight where Badi had fallen. My knees go weak. Following the trail of bloodstains, I creep under the bush to Saja's hiding place. A pang of fear shoots through my bones when I see her huddled there, cradling her brother's limp body in her arms.

Tears run down Saja's face. "Oh, my sweet Badi!" she moans. Blood drips from her fingers.

A sour taste rises to my throat as I examine the wound. It's so much deeper than I thought. I lower my ear to Badi's face to listen for breath. The air feels thick, oppressive. I strain to listen, my ears aching to hear something. The silence is painfully loud. Nothing. After several moments, I rest my head on Badi's chest and listen for the beat of his heart.

Saja and Jamal watch me, their faces white as phantoms, waiting for me to lift my head and tell them that Badi is just sleeping. But I do not rise, and Badi does not wake. In stunned silence, we listen to the noise of the men in the streets and the sound of a nightingale singing in the trees. When it seems ages have passed, I lift my head from Badi's chest. My arms and legs are heavy stones. I try to speak. My mouth is dry, but I croak out the words: "Saja, I'm so sorry—"

Saja stares at her brother's lifeless body.

I swallow past the lump in my throat. "Saja, we have to let the men find Badi. They'll take his body to the master of the baths, and he'll know what to do. We can't stay here or carry him ourselves." I move Badi's body out into the open as gently as I can. He looks Jamal's size. I stare at his skinned knees and tousled hair. The quivering in my chest moves to my stomach, and sickness rises to my throat. My eyes fill, and everything turns blurry as I creep back inside.

Saja shakes like she's holding back a rising flood. When I take her hand, the dam breaks. Sobs and tremors rack Saja's body as her words spill out in a torrent of convulsive whispers.

"No! My sweet Badi!" She wrenches her hand away from mine. "I never should have listened to you and let Badi meet your brother. You thought it would help keep him safe? You didn't even care. You never did. Why did you run off, right when Badi was hurt? Jamal was safe on the horse, but we needed you. Your brother's still alive, and now my brother's dead!"

I wrap my arms around Saja and pull her close; my tears slide down her heaving shoulder. But she stiffens and peels away my arms. The night feels suddenly cold. Moonlight dances over the ground as the branches of the bushes sway above them. The nightingale's song sounds sad and far away. I shiver as I listen to the men taking Badi away. "I'm so sorry," I whisper again.

Saja holds her hand up, staring at the blood, still wet, on her fingers. She turns to me and, without a word, slaps me hard across the face. Frozen in shock, I watch her crawl out of the bush and walk away without looking back.

14

I don't sleep all night. Jamal lies curled in my arms, weeping, as he clutches Badi's turban in his fists. By the time the cock crows, it seems our eyes have emptied themselves of an ocean. I rise and rinse my face. It isn't real. I just saw Badi yesterday, healthy and laughing with Jamal. His death is a dream. A nightmare.

The water trickles off my cheeks in red drops like bloody tears. Badi's blood from Saja's hand. My whole body starts shaking as I stare at the water in the basin. A wrenching pain twists my insides. Saja's pain must be a thousand times worse. Why didn't I rush to her when I first saw her crying there with Badi? I might have been able to save him. The thought weighs on me like a pile of bricks; I can hardly breathe from the pressure. Remembering the sting of Saja's slap and the coldness that settled over me as she walked away makes me weep fresh tears.

I hunger for the tiniest words of forgiveness from her, but I dread being turned away like a guilty criminal. My reflection in the water glares back at me. I take the basin and throw the water at the shutter screens. Some of it flies out the window and the rest drips down the screens and the wall, making a puddle on the floor.

Brisk knocking on the front door pulls me from my thoughts. Slaves don't have the freedom of mourning. With swollen eyes and hair matted to my head, I open the door and squint into bright sunlight. I mumble a greeting to Leila, who's returning her sister-in-law's measure in an even brighter mood than the day before. But when Leila sees my red eyes, she catches hold of my sleeve.

"What's wrong, dear? Oh!" She reaches out and holds

my chin and cheek. "What a nasty cut. Are you all right?"

I wince at her tender touch. I forgot about the wound from Stinger's ring. I nod and pull my scarf down lower. *What would it feel like to rest my head on the shoulder of a woman like Leila and tell her everything?* If only I had Umi. Mother's words would be like a healing potion.

I take the measure. "I'm fine. As-salaam alaykum."

The moment the door closes, Mistress flies from her chamber and snatches the measure from my hands. "Let me see that!" she cries. Her eyes widen as she inspects the underside of the cup. I want to slip back to my mat before Mistress can think of an early morning chore for me.

But a bleating sound escapes Mistress's throat, and she sinks to her knees.

Thinking she's fainting, I rush to catch her, but Mistress only stares, horrified, at the measure. I peer over her shoulder. On the bottom of the cup, stuck to the cooking fat, is a shiny gold coin.

I gasp.

At that moment, Master enters the hallway. His mouth

falls open when he sees his wife sobbing on the floor. "What is the meaning of this?" he demands.

Mistress wails louder than a funeral mourner. "Ali Baba is already far richer than you!" She pulls the coin off the fat. "He doesn't count his gold—he *measures* it!" She plunks the coin into the cup and shakes the measure at her husband like a tambourine.

Master's face turns pale when he sees the shiny evidence. He plucks the gold from the cup. His eyes look as if they might pop from his head. "The fortune-teller's prediction is coming true," he murmurs. "Ali Baba grows rich, while I am meant to lose my wealth? I won't let this happen." He squeezes the coin in his fist and curses. "Marjana! Go fetch my brother immediately, before he leaves for the forest."

I drag my eyes away from the coin and nod to Master. There's no way Abu-Zayed could have known this would happen if he made the whole thing up. I hurry out of the house and catch up with Leila just as she reaches her door. "As-salaam alaykum!" I practically shout at the woman. "Master must speak with Ali Baba immediately—it's an urgent matter. He's quite upset."

Leila hurries inside to fetch her husband, who appears at the door moments later, blinking in surprise. I don't see lazy Rasheed anywhere, of course. At least I don't have to face him again.

As soon as I return to the house with Ali Baba, Master bustles him into a nearby room and slams the door. Mistress drops the measure. Her hands fly to her face as she hurries from the room. Cook scurries to the back of the house, but I'm not going anywhere. Something strange is happening—I can feel it in my bones. I pick up the measure and stand in the hallway, listening to the voices behind the door.

"Ali Baba, you deceive me!" Master thunders. "You pretend to be a poor Sufi, turning away from worldly wealth and devoting yourself to Allah, but you secretly measure gold as if it were grain! What is the meaning of this?"

I step closer to the door to hear Ali Baba's soft answer.

"Brother, it's a wonder, to be sure. You're right—I am no

longer poor. My fortune has changed, praise Allah! But I don't need worldly wealth; I can use it to help others!"

"What? I demand you tell me everything."

"I'll gladly tell you the story. It's an astonishing one, I assure you. It happened just two days ago, when I was at the edge of the forest, cutting wood. I saw what looked like an army approaching on horseback in a cloud of dust. Fearing they were robbers, I climbed the nearest tree for safety. I counted forty—all rough-looking men, armed with scimitars and knives."

"The Forty Thieves!" Master cries.

I almost gasp out loud and have to cover my mouth with my hand.

"Yes, brother. The finest-looking one among them, who I took to be their leader, made his way through the bushes below me till he reached a rocky slope. I could hardly believe what happened next."

"Hurry and tell me, then! You try my patience, Ali Baba."

"'Open, Sesame!'" Ali Baba cries.

For a few moments, everything is quiet, till Master's voice erupts, "Open *what*? Have you been eating hashish?"

"I'm in my right mind, brother. The captain said those very words, 'Open, Sesame,' and a door opened in the rocks!"

"No!"

"Yes!"

I can't believe what I'm hearing. There are no such things as magic words. *Open, Sesame.* The idea is absurd. Ali Baba has always seemed so simple, so ignorant, but now he's trying to dupe his own brother? Maybe he's like the tricksters on the streets.

Ali Baba continues his story in an animated voice. "The robbers went inside the cave, and the door shut by itself. I waited in the tree to see what would happen. Finally, the door opened, and the thieves returned. After the captain said, 'Close, Sesame,' they mounted their horses and rode away. A great gust of wind almost knocked me out of the tree as soon as they were gone. It practically blew me to the rock face where the entrance had appeared and disappeared moments ago, and I decided to enter it myself. I had to see what was inside this enchanted cave! I inspected every inch of the rock but could find no door or device. But as soon as I spoke the magic words, the door flew open, and I saw the most amazing chamber, brightly lit, and full of the most thrilling treasures you could imagine!"

Impossible. I can barely keep from laughing out loud. Ali Baba's tale is rich—better than the professional storytellers on the streets of Baghdad. Somehow, he's managed to get a fortune—no wonder he was so excited the night I saw him hurrying home with his loaded donkeys—but a magic cave? No, Ali Baba must be a swindler. Or a thief.

A small gasp of surprise near my elbow makes me jump. Jamal crouches beside me, his ear glued to the door. His eyes are red and swollen from crying for Badi.

"What are you doing here, you little donk—"

"Shh!" Jamal puts his finger to his lips.

Ali Baba's talking eagerly. "Can you believe it? There

was a splendid table set with the choicest of foods and the rarest of delicacies. There was enough to feed a hundred street urchins! Everywhere I looked I saw rich silks and brocades, colorful rugs—even magic carpets that flew around the room. Pearls, emeralds, rubies, heaps of gold and silver, and leather purses of money littered the floor."

Aha! So Ali Baba's jangling baskets were full of those gold coins that day he was hurrying up the street with his donkeys! I can imagine Master's greedy eyes glittering with envy of such a find.

"Think of all the poor people we could help with such wealth!" Ali Baba goes on. "I have such plans for it—an orphanage and a school for the homeless children who roam the streets. Oh, the possibilities are endless. I brought out as many bags of gold as my donkeys could carry, and on a whim, I caught one of the magic carpets and brought it out as well. Then I said, 'Close, Sesame,' and hurried home, praising Allah all the way!"

Jamal squeezes my hand, his eyes lighting up as he listens. I sigh. Everyone hears the legends of treasure hoards. There are even professionals who spend their lives hunting for such fortunes. Maybe Ali Baba really did stumble upon the Forty Thieves' hoard by accident, but why is he making up this crazy story about magic words and flying rugs?

"Humph." Master sounds impatient. "I've seen a bit of your gold. Show me the carpet."

Silence.

"Well?"

"I'm afraid you would be disappointed. Though the carpet flew when it was in the cave, it has lain quite still on the floor since I brought it home. But I—"

"Enough of these fantasies. I believe you've found a great stash of gold—too much for the likes of you—and I demand that you tell me what you plan to do."

"Brother," Ali Baba says, "you should have a share in this good fortune. It is too great a responsibility for just one man to manage."

"Well, I would expect so!" says Master. "But you must tell me where to find this cave!"

I roll my eyes. Doesn't Ali Baba know that his brother will take advantage of him if he reveals the location of his newfound wealth?

"Certainly, brother," Ali Baba answers in a kind voice. "We must keep this secret for fear of our lives, but I have nothing to hide from you."

I almost drop the measure. Why would he agree to such a thing? Master would do almost anything, I think, to prevent the fortune-teller's predictions from coming true, including stealing from his own brother.

Cook calls for me and Jamal. I grab my brother's ear and pull him away from the door. "You can't say anything about this to anyone. Do you understand?"

"A magic treasure cave!" Jamal whispers.

"Shh! There's no such thing as magic."

Cook yells again with the hint of a whipping in her voice.

Jamal wiggles free. "You're still not my master," he says as soon as he escapes. He sticks his tongue out.

A flash of pain and anger sweeps over me, and my

words burst out before I can rein them in. "If I were your master, I would have kept you home last night so you wouldn't have gotten Badi killed!"

Jamal freezes. His face drains of its color, reminding me of the way he looked the night the devil-man burst through the door. As soon as I say them, the words sting like poison on my tongue. "Jamal, wait—" But before I can stop him, he turns and flies down the corridor to the kitchen.

I slide to the floor and hug my knees. Everything's collapsing. I long to clutch my fate tightly in my own hands, but everyone keeps prying away my fingers. I want to be strong for Jamal and myself, to get us what we want, what we need. But I don't know exactly what that is anymore.

Ali Baba's voice lowers as he tells Master how to find the cave, and I can't hear what he's saying. But soon I hear both men approaching the door, and I hurry to hide around the corner as Master shuffles Ali Baba into the hallway and to the front door.

"A very interesting story, indeed!" Master says. "Brother, you must tell no one else of this tale. I will take care of everything, you just leave this to me! Now, off you go—I have many things to do."

And he shoves Ali Baba lightly out the door and closes it behind him. As soon as he is gone, Master chuckles to himself and says under his breath, "Fool."

When I turn to leave the hall, he hears me and says, "Marjana, go tell your mistress to come see me immediately—I have important news to tell her!" He rubs his hands together, a glint in his eye. "Hurry! I need to leave soon."

"Yes, Master," I say, and hurry to find her.

15

As evening draws near, Mistress grows uneasy. Nothing I say seems to help. Making matters worse, Master doesn't return home by his usual time. Mistress won't stop pacing between the front door and the window, wringing her hands as if trying to squeeze water from them. Still he doesn't come home.

I sit by the window, thinking of Saja. *Will Allah listen to me?* I can't even think of the right words to pray. Umi's Twirling Song comes to mind. If I could spin straight to Allah, I would ask Him to send His angels to comfort Saja tonight.

By the time the sky turns purple and gold along the

horizon, Mistress's eyes are puffy from crying. "Marjana!" she finally cries, "Escort me to my brother-in-law's house—I must speak with him."

Something's gone horribly wrong. Mistress is high-strung, but this is worse than usual. I take her trembling arm and walk with her the short distance to Ali Baba's home. When the couple sees Mistress in such distress, they immediately pull us into the house.

"What is it, sister-in-law?" Ali Baba's brows wrinkle together. "Where's my brother?"

"Oh, Ali Baba! Forgive him—he's done a wicked thing. He left this morning for the cave to swindle you of all the treasure," she cries. "I'm afraid he's in danger. The sun is setting, and he hasn't returned!"

I brace Mistress, who seems ready to faint. Ali Baba jumps to life. "I'll ready the donkeys. I must hurry!"

Leila pulls Mistress to the other room to comfort her.

Rasheed is lounging on his pillows again, his long legs draped over a fancy new carpet—it must be the rug Ali Baba took from the cave and swore was magic. It's pretty, but definitely ordinary. Rasheed should leap to his feet and hurry to the cave with his father, but the young man remains seated. His humble garments are made of wool, yet his proud face is fierce as a tiger's. He looks like an annoying prince who would have all the silly princesses fawning like kittens. I roll my eyes as I glance away from him.

How can he treat his family like this? He should realize how fortunate he is to even have people who love him and take care of him. If he were my brother, I'd wrestle him to the floor and tell him exactly what I think. I clench my fists to hold in the brewing anger, but it doesn't work. "What's wrong with you?" My words burst out like steam from a kettle. "All you do is lie around. Don't you care about your father or your uncle?"

Rasheed looks stricken. His nostrils flare, and his face twists as if he's in great pain. He gropes among his cushions till he finds a carved wooden rod. I flinch. *Would he dare beat me with that?* He struggles to push his legs into place, and with great effort, he positions himself against the rod and attempts to rise to his feet.

My heart leaps to my throat. Rasheed can do no such thing. "Wait! I didn't know—" My face burns like hot coals.

"You're right!" Rasheed shouts. "All I do is lie around. I need to *do* something!"

"But you're . . . you're . . ."

"I'm lame!" Rasheed throws the rod across the room in frustration and falls back onto the cushions.

At that moment, Ali Baba returns. "My son," he says, "your legs are weak, but your mind is strong." He picks up the cane and hands it back to Rasheed. "I need you to help me tonight." He pulls the young man to his feet, supporting one side, while Rasheed steadies himself with the cane. "Stay at my brother's house and watch for my return. You must pray to Allah for your uncle and me. Recite the Qur'an over my brother's household for protection, and sing some qasida to occupy them and keep their minds at peace."

Rasheed stands up straighter. "Yes, Father."

The women return to the room, Mistress's eyes wet and red.

"We must hurry." Ali Baba turns to me. "Help us get Rasheed to my brother's house—I will need to gather oil and lamps there."

But before I can object, Ali Baba moves aside for me to take his place beside Rasheed. I put my arm around the young man's waist. Women don't put their arms around men. Why isn't Rasheed outraged, and how could devout Ali Baba order me to do such a thing?

Rasheed can use his legs a little, but it's an obvious burden for him. He puts most of his weight on the rod so as not to lean on me too heavily. Despite his inability to walk, he doesn't lack in strength and his arm feels solid. The smell of ginger and roasted lamb lingers on his clothes. Jamal will be this big one day. I wish I hadn't spoken so harshly to Rasheed. I never should have believed the rumors about him being lazy. At least I have my scarf, which hides the shame on my face.

Together, we walk back to Master's house. Leila

supports Mistress in the same way I hold Rasheed, and Ali Baba leads the donkeys. Once there, Ali Baba goes in search of the oil lamps as I lead Rasheed to the floor cushions and gather Cook and Jamal. Rasheed clears his throat and addresses everyone. "My father wishes me to recite the Qur'an for protection and sing qasida for your pleasure until he returns from his night journey. He put me in charge of the household until your master arrives."

When all is quiet, he bows his head and closes his eyes. After several moments of silence, he lifts his head and begins the recitation. His eyes light up as he sings the holy words; his face comes alive.

I've only heard the Qur'an recited in turns, by groups of men, not just one. *Has he memorized the whole thing?* Until now, the words of the Qur'an always shot past me, aiming for the hearts of masters, not slave girls. But it never sounded so much like a song before.

Even Mistress stops crying and wipes her eyes, listening as if in a trance. Leila whispers into Mistress's ear, "Shaykh Al-Junayed visits him almost every day with lessons. The shaykh says Rasheed is blessed by Allah. My son longs with all his heart to attend a madrasa and become a teacher, but his legs make it impossible."

Restless, I drift toward the back of the house, looking for Ali Baba. The haunting sound of Rasheed's voice follows me through the house. I find Ali Baba lighting the lamps.

"Marjana, you and I must leave for the cave immediately!"

"Me?"

Ali Baba nods firmly. "Yes, Marjana. Rasheed would volunteer, of course, but he is not able, and I truly need him here to keep the household calm and at peace. You've proved yourself most capable to do what I ask. Please. I need your help."

I still can't believe the cave is magic, but if the part about the Forty Thieves is true, going to their cave is the last thing I want to do. I never want to see the devil-man again. But I can't let Ali Baba make the journey alone. I nod gravely.

Dusk is falling as I follow Ali Baba through the woods. We come to the edge of a small clearing. After we're certain that the thieves are nowhere about, Ali Baba and I step out into the open and stand before a stone cliff face. It looks exactly like an ordinary cliff face—nothing remarkable. Certainly no door cut into it. I wonder what's wrong with Ali Baba. It seems only a child or a simpleton could believe that behind this rock hides a magical cave full of treasure.

"Are you ready, Marjana?"

Ali Baba's eyes have a wild look about them. Is he mad? I swallow hard and nod my head, wondering if he has lost his senses. "Open, Sesame!" he cries.

At Ali Baba's words, the ground shakes. Pebbles and earth cascade down the wall of rock, and a great door slowly opens. My jaw drops in awe.

Magic.

It's true.

I feel dizzy as we step inside.

Light flickers on the cave walls, but when I pick up a

lamp, it's empty—it burns without oil! I hold it in front of me and gaze around the room in amazement. Heaps of gold coins cover the cave floor, and in the center, a great table is set with an elaborate feast of steaming roasted meats, sparkling goblets of drink, jewellike fruits, and delicate pastries. It's the magic never-ending banquet that Jamal told me about the night we were taken by the Forty Thieves, and I didn't believe him. He was right. It's all real. Luxurious tapestries lie over chests brimming with gems and jewels. Most amazing of all, a flying carpet floats around the cave, above our heads, just as Ali Baba said.

I stagger around the room in wonder, scooping up the gold pieces to make sure they're real and letting them fall through my hands like water. Am I dreaming? I must be. But I could never dream up something so extravagant as this. It is only when my eye catches the gleaming pile of scimitars that I remember why we are here. In my distraction, I have lost track of time, and a nervous flutter rises in my chest as I scan the cave for

Ali Baba. I spot him huddled over in a dark corner.

"Ali Baba," I whisper. "Where is . . . Master?"

When he turns to me, Ali Baba's face is the color of ash. He points to four bundles he has wrapped and placed on the ground. "Here is the body of your master, my brother."

The horror of his words strikes me dumb.

Ali Baba covers his face with his hands. "I found him like this . . . quartered. . . ."

My knees turn weak. I place my hand on the trembling man's thin shoulder. "I'm sorry, Ali Baba."

"The thieves murdered my brother, quartered his body, and left it here."

I shiver, staring at the bundles he wrapped in pieces of elegant cloth, and then I freeze. More of the fortune is coming true: When Master said he was twice the man Ali Baba was, Abu-Zayed had said, *Be that as it may—in the end, you will be but a quarter of the man he is.*

"Ali Baba, if we don't hurry and leave, they may come back and do the same thing to us!"

"Marjana." He takes my hand. "I need your help with

my brother's remains. I believe you're brave enough to do as I ask."

I nod.

"When the robbers see my brother's body is missing, they'll realize someone knows their secret. They'll be looking for news of a murdered man's funeral. We must make it seem as if he died in his bed at home, or we're all in danger."

Remembering the devil-man's serpent tattoo makes me want to sink to the floor.

"I understand. I'll take care of . . ." I glance at the bundles on the ground. "I'll take care of everything."

16

The following morning while Mistress sleeps, I stick gold pieces from the cave into my sash and hurry with Jamal to the bathhouse. I have a plan to make it seem like Master died in bed, but before I can do anything, I need to see Saja. The aching guilt I feel for Badi's death is too much to bear another day. When we reach the bathhouse, it isn't open yet. Saja will be working with the other servant girls in the courtyard, doing the laundry.

Jamal scowls at the ground, kicking stones in the road as we near the gate. I try taking his hand, but he yanks it back.

"Leave me alone."

Lately he's pulling away from me, like a thread unraveling from a garment. If I don't do something, I'll lose him completely and feel more cold and alone than I already do.

"Jamal, you were right."

He stops and kicks a rock toward me, almost hitting my shin. "About what?"

"About everything. That I'm not your master and I'm just a slave. You were right about Red Beard—he won't want you to ride with him now that I made you leave. And the magic—you were right about that, too."

Jamal looks up in surprise at that, a glimmer of interest in his eyes, but quickly turns away again. He hasn't forgiven me yet.

I dig a rock loose with the toe of my sandal and kick it between Jamal's feet. "But I was right about some things. I was right to want to keep you from joining the gangs. I may not have done all the right things, but I was right to want to stop you, Jamal, and you know it."

He frowns at the rock near his foot.

"But I was wrong about something important."

He steps on the rock, pressing it into the dirt.

"I was wrong when I said it was your fault that Badi died. I was sad and angry. I threw those words at you when I should have just thrown them away, because they aren't true. It isn't your fault, Jamal."

He keeps his eyes on the stone. "Then whose fault is it?"

I stare at the rock, too. Tears rise to my eyes. "Badi chose to do what he did on his own, but he didn't realize how dangerous it was. Neither of you did." The burden of a hundred stones in my heart starts to lift. "He just wanted to be a brave warrior and stop the boys from hurting you."

My heart lightens just a fraction at the truth of my own words. Badi's death isn't my fault, either.

"You would have done the same thing for him, wouldn't you?"

Jamal nods and picks up the stone. "Badi tried to help me just like Saja helped you. Because that's what friends do."

The truth in his words is a mixture of bitter herbs and sweet honey. Just when I finally open my heart to Saja's friendship, I've lost it.

As Jamal and I near the courtyard entrance of the bathhouse, a hulking khādim guard walks his rounds past the locked gate. A ring with a key on it hangs from his belt. I pull my brother close enough to whisper in his ear.

"Jamal, listen. Badi was brave. And what I'm going to ask you to do for me and his sister is brave, too. Listen." I tell him my plan and watch his eyes light up as he listens. He nods, and as soon as I'm done, he skips off toward the guard, and I follow.

When Jamal stops short in front of the surprised guard, tripping him, I have the key off the ring before the man even finishes cursing. As soon as he's gone, we burst out laughing. It feels good—I haven't smiled in ages. But when I turn toward the bathhouse courtyard and unlock the gate, the feeling fades. There's a stone in the pit of my stomach. I can't bear to see Saja only to have her curse me or slap me again like she did before. I don't know what to say to her.

I pull my brother aside. "I can't go in, Jamal."

"But she's your friend like Badi was my friend."

"I know." My voice wavers. "But I don't know if she wants to see me, yet. Here—take this to her and tell her it's from me." I hand Jamal a cracked cardamom, which Leila said means *I am in agony.*

"It's just a seed pod." Jamal wrinkles his nose. "And it's broken."

I touch my cheek where Saja slapped me. "I know it's broken. Just go." I give him a little push and hide behind the bathhouse wall, watching.

Jamal hurries to Saja, who's wringing out washed linens and hanging them in the sun to dry. After talking for a little while, Jamal hands Saja the cracked cardamom. I strain to see Saja's expression, but she's too far away.

All at once, Saja turns and runs from the courtyard. My

spirits sink, but Jamal stands still, as if waiting for her return. It seems ages before she comes running back and hands something to him.

My heart flutters with hope. As soon as Jamal joins me on the road, I take hold of his shoulders. "What did she say?"

Jamal shrugs my hands off. "Not much. She was crying."

"What did she *say*, little donkey?"

"I asked her if she had heard any news about Red Beard. She said he's gone. The bathhouse boys say he's away on a journey, and all the gangs are quiet."

I cross my arms and bite my lip to keep from crying. "That's all?"

"And she gave you another stupid present." Jamal presses a small seed into my palm.

Shaking, I wait for my heart to resume its normal rhythm, but it doesn't. I slowly open my fist. I almost fall to my knees when I see what's inside.

A pear seed.

I let it drop from my fingers into the dirt and stare out at the streets of Baghdad with a lump in my throat.

I hate you.

"What's wrong?" Jamal squints at me. "Let's go—Cook will whip me if I'm not there to help her make breakfast."

I blink at him, forcing back the tears. "I have an errand to do for Ali Baba; you go on without me."

Jamal shrugs and darts away until he disappears in the crowd. Then I let the tears fall freely behind my scarf.

Finally, I pull myself together and dry my eyes.

Ali Baba is counting on me, and I have a lot to do. First, the apothecary shop. If my plan doesn't work, none of us will be safe from the Forty Thieves. As I make my way through the crowds and street performers, I step around the old storyteller, who sits cross-legged on the ground near a fruit vendor's stall. His eyes are closed, and he has the same look of concentration on his face as Rasheed wore when he prepared to recite the Qu'ran.

Perhaps he might know Abu-Zayed. Fortune-tellers and storytellers of the streets frequent the same places and often share the same customers. Some folks claim they even sell the same wares—fiction. But maybe Abu-Zayed isn't a falsifier after all. My heart starts thumping wildly. He knew that Ali Baba would become wealthy and Master would be killed. Maybe Abu-Zayed knows what's going to happen next.

I slip a gold dinar from my sash and drop it onto the storyteller's lap. "As-salaam alaykum."

The little man's eyes pop open, and he scoops up the coin. He squints, holding it just inches from his face. "Wa alaykum as-salaam! I just had a dream," he mumbles. "About an ancient coin, just like this one, and of its many brothers hidden away all these years! Gifts from the jinn, they were."

I hope he is talking about good jinn, not the harmful ones.

"Sir." I clear my throat.

The storyteller raises his eyes. "And you were in the dream as well! Ah, I knew you'd come back to hear my story." The man's thin shoulders shake as he cackles to himself.

I smile at him. "Sir, the coin is yours to keep." I glance around the square and lower my voice. "I hope you might tell me where I can find the fortune-teller Abu-Zayed? It's very important." I'm nervous to be asking about a fortune-teller in public, but the storyteller doesn't seem shocked one bit.

The man's gnarled fingers curl around the coin. "Yes, yes, the fortune-teller is nearby. He shows up when he is needed. But now I am here, and I have a story for you."

"But I have very little time—" I start to protest, but falter when I look into his eyes. The way he smiles at me makes me hesitate. Something feels so familiar about it.

"It's a very short story—it will be over and done with before you realize it. Besides, this one is about a man you know."

My mouth falls open. "A man I know? Who is it?"

"It's a man we all know because we *are* this man. He is

our brother, our wife, our lover, our friend. He is a slave girl, a poor man, a thief, and a captain. Today, he is a merchant."

My skin prickles at the storyteller's strange words. I wait, holding my breath.

The storyteller licks his lips and begins. "One morning, perhaps it was not long ago, a certain merchant was strolling down this very street. As he walked along, his head was full of plans for the future and his heart was full of his own desires. Well, you can imagine his surprise when he turned the street corner and came face-to-face with Death! It was an odd sort of meeting. Death merely stood there with a strange look on his face and stared at the merchant.

"Needless to say, the merchant did not stand around! He flew like the wind from the place, hoping to put much distance between himself and Death. He traveled all day, as swiftly as he could, and arrived at a faraway town by nightfall. Weary from his long journey, he entered the town. But who do you think was there to meet him at the city gates? Death was there, waiting for him all along."

The storyteller's eyes grow keen and he gives me a crooked grin. "Do you know why Death gave the merchant such a strange look that morning?"

I shake my head.

"Why, it was because Death was surprised to see the merchant in his hometown, as he had an appointment with him far away in the foreign town that evening!" He gives a disdainful laugh.

"Oh!" I cry out in dismay. "The man tried to escape his fate—and that's the very thing that led him to it! What an awful story." It's just like Master's death. I wince. He, too, tried to defy his fortune, yet no matter what Master did, however he tried to defy it, every turn he took only led him to the same place fate had intended for him from the beginning.

The storyteller shrugs. "The threads of fate are woven in such an intricate way; some find beauty in their design. I myself find satisfaction in using fate for my own purposes." A thin smirk creeps across his features, reminding me of the way Abu-Zayed had grinned at me through the gap in the curtains.

I gasp. "You're the fortune-teller!"

CHAPTER

17

I'd been distracted by the storyteller's tattered, smelly clothes and comical gestures, but now I see that he and the formidable fortune-teller are definitely one and the same. I can even see the tip of the jagged scar on his neck.

I'd wanted to confront the man, but now that he's here in front of me, my bones turn weak and fear consumes me.

"People aren't always what they seem, eh, bathhouse boy?"

My face flushes and my heart races. How did he recognize me—my voice, my eyes?

"But—" My hands flutter to my scarf. "You disguise yourself so you don't get caught telling fortunes! At least I had good reasons for my disguise."

"We all have our reasons." Abu-Zayed says. "Mine is a long story. A story about a thief. I will tell you the short version. A young man once coveted a secret that belonged to me. He wanted it so much he followed me to the edge of the forest and killed me. Then he stole my secret away."

"He *killed* you?" Maybe the man isn't a fortune-teller after all. Maybe he just isn't quite right in the head. Scores of poor people living on the streets of Baghdad talk to themselves and mutter nonsense—maybe Abu-Zayed is like them. Sighing, I turn to go, but the man catches the hem of my garment. I hesitate.

Abu-Zayed points to the jagged scar on his neck. "Oh yes, he killed me." He laughs in scorn. "At least, that's what *he* thinks. I hid because the jinn told me to. They've always been my faithful guides. When they listened to the plans of the angels and heard my name whispered on the winds, they hurried to me right away and told me what to do."

I can't decide if Abu-Zayed is crazy or not, but the thought of him truly conversing with evil jinn makes my blood run cold. "You should not have meddled in the fate of my master and Ali Baba."

"Don't tell me that your master didn't deserve it. And Ali Baba! What a simpleton. He's always greeted me every day on his way to the forest and gives me the crusts of his own bread, the poor fool."

"He does?" Ali Baba seems different than anyone I have ever met. The old man's gaze softens. The wildness leaves his features, and once again, I recognize the old storyteller. "It's true the angels are weaving all our fates together, but the threads are our own. The fortune-teller in me would say grab ahold of their strands and wring everything you can from them. 'Tis the course I have chosen and I cannot change now. It is too late for me," he says with a sigh. "But the storyteller in me says this: Whatever the angels are creating out of your threads, make sure it's strong and beautiful, eh? That's all I can say to you. We shall soon see what comes of it all."

Abu-Zayed closes his eyes, and the look of concentration settles over his features once again. "As-salaam alaykum," he murmurs.

"But, sir—" I hardly know what to say, but it's obvious the man is finished talking. "Wa alaykum as-salaam," I reply as I drop a coin in Abu-Zayed's lap and turn away, moving through the market square in a daze. What did he say about the threads of people's fates being woven together by the angels?

Make sure it's strong and beautiful, eh?

What kind of fortune-telling is that? But then again, Master's fortune is definitely coming true. The thought of my dead Master jolts me out of my trance. I still have an important task that must be done early. When Master's death is announced, everyone in Baghdad must be made to think he died in his bed at home. If the thieves hear about a murdered man's funeral, they'll find out Ali Baba took his body from the cave and the devil-man will come find them. It's my job to keep that from happening. I pick up my pace and head to the apothecary.

Saja told me about the brother and sister who own the shop and how the woman trades plants and seeds for Saja's help. Cook talks about the owners as well, saying they can always be counted on for the latest gossip. From the condition of a neighbor's foot rash to the state of the imam's wart problems, all manner of personal health information is shared freely by the shop owners.

I push open the door to the tinkling sound of little bells. Light streams through the cut designs in the wooden screens, casting strange shadows over the clay jars and glass bottles of powders, pills, syrups, and ointments that clutter the shelves. Dried roots and herbs hang from the ceiling, and vats of scented oil line the walls. Breathing inside the apothecary shop is like being drugged with a potion. The air hangs thick with the perfume of spices—henna, thyme, garlic, rosemary. The heady scents bring a sharp pang as I recall Saja's dream of owning a perfume shop. I force myself to swallow back tears. While I had the chance, I should have told Saja how much it meant to me that she trusted me with her secrets.

I wait at the counter near a large set of scales and a stone mortar and pestle. The brother and sister soon emerge from the back room, their faces beaming. Kadir sports a turban that towers like a sultan's. Kadira brings with her the scent of roses and rain, making the whole room smell like a garden in spring.

"As-salaam alaykum." I bow my head.

"Wa alaykum as-salaam!" they exclaim in unison.

"I'm Marjana—"

"Ah, Marjana! We've heard of you. Welcome; my name is Kadira and this is my brother, Kadir."

"My master—"

"Oh, we know your master," Kadir says knowingly. His turban sways as he speaks. "We've heard *all* about your mistress, too."

I smile. Cook's tongue must be just as loose as the shop owners'. I start to pose a question, but Kadira asks eagerly, "Have you heard about Old Ghayda?"

I shake my head. "I don't know Ghayda."

She throws her hands into the air. "What a melancholy temperament."

"So irritable!" adds Kadir.

"Her husband's at his wits' end," Kadira continues. "Ghayda can't sleep, which means *he* can't sleep!"

Kadir shakes his head, and his turban rocks precariously. "Too much black bile in her body."

"If only she'd eat the pickled peppers I gave her and soak at the baths every day, her humors would balance themselves out and she could get a little rest!"

"And her husband, too."

"Maybe it's her cooking," Kadira whispers, even though we are the only ones in the shop. "I hear her bread's dry and hard as a stone."

I let out a little moan. "Oh! If only my poor master had such mild ailments as this Ghayda! His problems are *so* much worse than hers."

Kadir's and Kadira's eyebrows rise at the same time. "What's the matter?" They lean forward, eyes wide.

"Well, he's—"

Before I can answer, Kadira interrupts. "Well, he's obviously choleric—anyone can tell by his sallow skin and his blustery voice."

"Too much yellow bile." Kadir clucks his tongue.

"Why, yes," I say. "And—"

"He drinks too much dry wine and eats too much overcooked mutton." Kadira folds her arms in front of her chest and frowns.

"You certainly know my master," I admit. "And now I'm afraid he's dangerously ill. His throat is dry and painful. His chest burns, and he coughs all the time. His fever's so high, he's turned delirious, and we don't know what to do!"

The brother and sister glance at each other triumphantly. "Choleric!" they declare. "Just as we thought."

Kadira scurries over to the shelves and starts collecting bottles.

Kadir lectures me as he assists his sister. "Darkness! You must keep him in the shade, where it's cooler. And don't forget melons! Make him eat as many as he can. The juicier the better."

Before long, they prepare some elixirs to bring down fever and a bag of twisted pieces of violet candy, intended to ease Master's supposed sore throat.

The shop owners send me on my way with mixed advice on balancing my own humors. Kadir feels I am too phlegmatic and need to eat salt in front of an open oven, while Kadira claims I am overly sanguine and should nibble mint leaves and sleep under an open window. As I leave the apothecary, I pop one of the sweets into my mouth from the bag of lozenges and smile to myself.

— ◈ —

Later that afternoon, I chop an onion until my eyes turn red and teary and then hurry back to the shop. I burst through the door, the bells jingling.

"Oh, help me!" I cry.

When the shop owners see my weepy eyes, their mouths fall open. Kadir drops the pestle he is holding; it falls with a thud to the floor. Kadira, who was pouring some seeds into his mortar, stares at me in stunned surprise as the seeds keep spilling from her bag, all over the mortar and counter.

"What is it?" they ask, their eyes wide and eager.

"My master." I sniff. "He is at death's door."

Kadir and Kadira blink at each other.

"I knew it!" Kadir exclaims.

"I thought so!" says Kadira.

Kadir nods to his sister, who takes a potion bottle off the shelf. He turns to me. "In sad times like these, there is only one thing we can do." He tries to make his voice sound somber, but his eyes are bright, and I think he must be imagining the thrill he will have in telling the next customer about my poor master and his dangerous, deathly disease.

Kadira hands me the bottle. "One drop will ease the pain of dying and bring days of deep, peaceful sleep, almost like death itself." She smiles. "It sounds lovely, doesn't it?"

I sniff again and wipe my eyes. "Thank you! I'm so

glad he won't have to suffer any longer."

"Yes!" they say together. "We are, too!" And though they try to make their faces sad, their voices ring out cheery and bright, as if they have picked out a fancy present for me to give to Master.

I nod and leave the shop. That should do the trick! The story of Master's "dangerous illness" is sure to be all over the neighborhood by evening prayer time.

18

The next day, I scrub the kitchen floor as I think over my plan. Soon we'll wash and enshroud Master's body and parade it through Baghdad for the funeral procession, and it's up to me to make sure no one suspects he was gruesomely murdered. I grimace at the thought of what I'll have to do.

As I wring the water from my rag, I hear music. But it sounds as if it's coming from inside the house rather than the street. Walking the corridor from the harem to the main room, I listen. It's Jamal's tabor, but who's accompanying him on a reed instrument? The notes undulate around the drum beats like a swaying dancer.

It hypnotizes, drawing me closer. The rhythm takes hold, stirring and fanning the cooled embers in my heart, my arms, my hips. I want to dance.

Peeking around the corner, I see Rasheed sitting on his rug and cushions, holding a long reed flute to his mouth. His eyes are closed, and his body sways to the music like a snake charmer's. His fingers pulsate against the holes in the flute, coaxing the notes to wake and leap into the air.

"Marjana, dance!" Jamal calls out when he sees me.

Rasheed opens his eyes and lowers his flute. He blinks as if coming out of a trance. "Do you dance? I didn't realize you and Jamal were so talented."

Jamal doesn't stop the rhythm but continues beating his drum as he speaks. "She loves to dance. Almost as much as playing her lute."

"The lute! We should all play music together sometime."

Why does Rasheed act kind to me despite the way I treated him? His eyes draw my trust toward him like iron to a lodestone. It scares me, but I don't want to pull myself away. I run my finger down the smooth surface of the flute. "What instrument is this?"

"It's called the ney. It's a sacred instrument to Sufis."

My heart leaps. I want so badly to learn more about my mother's beliefs. "My mother's master was a Sufi, and she practiced the same sacred rituals you do. But she died when I was young and my new master, your uncle, had different practices. I have always wanted to know more about what she believed. What exactly are Sufis?" I almost whisper the question, because I am ashamed at my ignorance.

Rasheed smiles, pleased at my interest. "Sufis are men and women who aren't satisfied with merely knowing *about* Allah; we seek the ecstasy of *knowing* Allah."

Jamal keeps drumming. The beats mirror my heartbeats, taking hold of them and dancing together inside my chest.

"One can know a thing in three different ways." Rasheed leans forward. "Take for instance a flame. You can be *told* of the flame."

Jamal's drumbeats get louder.

"And you can *see* the flame with your own eyes." Rasheed reaches toward the shelf and lifts the magic lamp that Ali Baba took from the cave. The light flickers, creating shadows over the wall behind them. The drumbeats pulse in my chest.

"And you can reach out and be *touched* by the flame." He raises his hand over the spout where the tongue of fire glows. He closes his eyes, and his eyebrows knot together as his palm passed slowly through the flame. When he opens his eyes, he smiles. "This is the way we Sufis seek to know Allah."

Jamal's drumbeats fill my whole body.

"Your music—does it help you know Allah in that way?"

Rasheed nods and glances at his ney. "Sometimes when I'm playing, the music feels like existence itself. There are some Sufis who do a whirling dance to the music. They say it brings them closer to Allah."

"The Twirling Song," I whisper. My heart seems made of feathers.

"The ecstasy comes when you get swept away with the rhythm, the movement, and you let go of yourself and understand your place in the world—your destiny. It is connecting with God." He raises the ney. "Would you like to dance?"

I can only nod. At that moment, I want to dance more than anything else in the world. The voice of Rasheed's flute joins the beat of Jamal's drum. I close my eyes and think of Umi dancing with me. I raise my arms in the air, letting the music turn me round and round until it lifts me out of myself, just as I remembered doing as a child.

The fingers of the breeze trail across my skin as if skimming the surface of deep water. It sends ripples of warmth through me as I let go and spin free of my body, free of the world. And it is liberating to feel so alive—to feel connected to everything, yet at the same time to be set loose from the things that bind me. I never thought I could feel this way again, but here I am.

I open my eyes, and everything's changed. Everything blends into one, and I'm a part of it all. I'm *free*.

When the music stops, I slip to the ground and watch the spinning world slow down.

"Marjana." Jamal's voice punctures my thoughts and swirls for a moment around my head. "Did you travel to Allah?" He stands over me, his eyes wide.

I wait as everything comes into focus and settles into place along with a contentment I've never felt before. The ache of Umi's absence is finally relieved by letting go of my desperate longing. I smile at Jamal and Rasheed. "I certainly traveled somewhere, though I never left the room."

Rasheed laughs. "That's the way I usually have to travel."

I rise, still dizzy from the dance, and smooth my qamis and sirwal.

"I would love to journey all over the world, but as you can see, I'm not a traveling man." Rasheed motions to his legs.

Jamal struts over and plops down beside him. "I've been all the way to Basra, once."

"Basra? That's a long way, indeed, little brother. An eight-day journey, at least. You've seen more of the world than I have."

Jamal puffs out his chest and grins. I smile at the words *little brother*. I wish Jamal had an older brother like Rasheed.

Rasheed sighs. "And yet, there's so much more of the world to see. It's almost impossible to envision how vast this universe is. Many people have tried, though, and through scientific study, we learn more and more every day. But what fantastical stories people have told in the past to describe the vastness! Remember the tale I was telling you about the king who was on a quest for the Ring of Solomon?"

Jamal nods, eagerly.

"The ancient tale goes that the king was given a tour of the universe and that it consisted of seven worlds."

Jamal's eyes widen.

"The seven worlds were carried by an angel. This angel stood on a rock that was placed on a giant bull, and the bull stood on a huge fish that was placed in an endless sea."

"Was that the bottom of the universe?" Jamal asks.

"Not even close! Below the sea, an endless space of air extended, and underneath the space was a realm of fire. Beneath that was the cosmic serpent who was so, so large, it could have swallowed all that was above it and not even know the difference."

Jamal whistles. "I bet the king was surprised that his universe was so big!"

Rasheed pats him on the back. "He was indeed. I imagine one day you too will do lots more traveling and go on adventures. You can come back and tell us true stories about what the world out there is really like." He laughs. "But don't get started too soon. We like having you around in our little part of the universe."

Jamal nods solemnly. "Don't worry. I don't have a map yet."

I laugh. "Better travel to the kitchen, little donkey. Cook will be home soon and she told you to start making the meatballs when she left for the market."

When Jamal runs off, Rasheed's grin turns into a more serious expression. "Marjana, I'm glad you are here because I wanted to talk to you." He motions for me to have a seat on the rug beside him.

I tense at his somber tone, but I sit down on the carpet.

"Marjana, my father told me about your plan for the funeral preparations tomorrow."

I frown. Obviously, he doesn't care for my idea and wants to take over. I fold my arms across my chest. Of course—I should have known.

"It's an excellent plan."

"Oh!" I uncross my arms, surprised.

Rasheed's eyebrows knot together. "But some people would lose their courage—or their stomachs—while overseeing such an ugly matter."

Is he being infuriating on purpose? I cross my arms again and lift my chin. "I have no intention of losing either."

Rasheed smiles. "I had a feeling you'd say something

like that. My father thinks you are a brave person, and I don't doubt it."

I can't figure him out—when I expect him to be cruel, he's kind. He speaks to me as an equal and doesn't order me around, even though his parents are my masters now. I'd like to stay and talk to him, but the thought makes me uncomfortable, as if I've forgotten to wear my headscarf. I turn to go. "I won't let your family down." I hardly know I've said the words before the promise is already hanging in the air between us. Feeling exposed, I pull my scarf down lower over my face.

"Marjana, don't go," he says. "I have complete faith in you. Father says it was your idea to use some of the treasure money to offer a reward through the magistrate for information leading to the captain's capture. He also says you took everything in stride the night he told you of my uncle and the cave."

My face turns hot and I stare at the swirling gold patterns on the crimson rug. The truth is far from what he supposes. I'm tired of holding bits of myself back and long to be known more fully. But it's hard. I take a deep breath and look at Rasheed. "To tell the truth, I was very much shaken. And . . . afraid. But I tried not to show it. I didn't believe your father before I saw it with my own eyes." I throw my hands up. "I still hardly know what to think."

"Yes, it's hard to believe some things until we experience them for ourselves. Take this carpet." He nods toward the rug we're sitting on. "My father says that when he arrived at the cave, this very rug was flying about as if it were alive. But the minute he left the cave with it, it became an ordinary rug. My father is a truthful man, and yet, it is difficult for me to imagine such a thing."

I run my hand over the soft weave of the fabric. "Perhaps it only does its magic inside the magic cave?"

"Perhaps. But the lamp continues to burn outside the cave."

"Maybe the carpet requires a magic rite to work, the

way that the cave opened only with the words 'Open, Sesame.'"

At that moment, the room seems to shift and fall away from us. I clutch the edge of the rug and cry out, "What's happening?"

19

The carpet lifts itself off the floor. Pillows tumble over the sides as it rises upward. I fall back and almost roll off, but Rasheed grabs my arm.

"You said the magic words!" He pulls me next to him in the center of the rug. "The words that worked for the cave work for the carpet, too!" The rug is halfway to the ceiling now, and still rising. "When the words opened the cave for Father, they must have brought the carpet to life." Rasheed's head bumps the ceiling and little crumbs of mud plaster fall off.

"How do we make it stop?" I can't hide the panic in

my voice. Rasheed and I press our palms against the ceiling and push, but the carpet keeps moving upward. If we don't get off soon, we'll be crushed. He won't be able to jump from the carpet like I can.

"Jump off, Marjana." Rasheed lies flat against the rug to give himself more space.

"But what about you?" I cry. We need more magic words. I have to bend my head and lie flat like Rasheed. I stare into his dark eyes. He's trying to mask his fear, but it's showing through. Suddenly his eyes light up as he realizes the same thing I do—we don't need to figure out the magic words to stop it. We already have them.

"Close, Sesame!" we yell at the same time.

The carpet slowly eases itself toward the floor and gently lands. For a moment, we stare at each other, our mouths hanging open. Then we burst out laughing. Rasheed sits up.

"If we can learn how to make this rug go where we want, I could become quite the traveling man after all."

He grins and strokes the fabric. "Maybe it obeys our thoughts, and we give it directions by simply thinking of where we want to go."

"But we wanted to go down, and it only went up. Maybe we have to say the commands out loud."

"Hold on, Marjana, I'm going to give it a try."

I roll onto my stomach and hold on.

"Open, Sesame."

The carpet starts to rise. When it lifts about a foot off the ground, Rasheed says, "Go forward."

But the carpet continues to rise.

"Take us around the room," Rasheed orders.

Still the carpet rises. There must be some other way to make the stubborn thing move. "Rasheed, try steering it with your hands, holding the edges."

Rasheed grabs the fringe on the front of the carpet in his fists. He slowly stretches the fringe away from him, and the rug eases forward. "You're right—it works!"

I hold on tighter. "Take us around the room."

"Ready?"

My heart beats out the answer *yes, yes, yes!* I nod as Rasheed pulls the fringe to the right and the carpet turns. We glide through the air past Jamal's drum and the magic lamp, and circle the entire room, smoother than a boat on a river. My heart, too, is flying high. The room's not large enough—we need more space. "Let's take it outside."

"If we hold the sides of the rug up, we can probably make it through the window."

We curl up the sides, hold them tightly, and Rasheed steers the rug through the open window. But as soon as we clear the sill, approaching footsteps sound from around the corner.

Rasheed whispers, "*Close, Sesame,*" and the carpet lands right as Cook rounds the corner with baskets full of food from the market. She stops abruptly and blinks at us. "How strange," she mumbles.

I jump to my feet. "Well, it was such a nice day, that I—I helped Master Rasheed set up his things outside."

"I can see that. But why on earth do you both have plaster on your heads?" Cook frowns and shakes her head as she goes inside.

I let out my breath. "Hurry—take us to the roof before someone else sees us."

Rasheed lifts us swiftly to the top of the house and lands there as we scan the streets below for people. No one's around.

I smile. "Now's your chance to see the city."

"But people might notice us." He turns in the direction of the mosque. "Besides, I must pray. Didn't you hear the call for prayers a moment ago?"

"Yes, that's perfect!" I glance toward the mosque. "Everyone's bowing in prayer and won't see our carpet in the sky. By the time your prayers are through, I'll have us too high for them to know what we are—if anyone notices us, they'll think we are a beautiful red bird soaring on the breeze."

Rasheed smiles. "I've never seen much of the city before." He pushes himself back, away from the front of the carpet, to give me room to navigate. "I never get to pray in the mosque—I think it must be even better to pray to Allah from the clouds."

This is real magic, right here within my grasp. I look over my shoulder at Rasheed. His head and chest are bowed low in prayer.

"Open, Sesame," I whisper.

The carpet rises from the roof, floating upward like steam from a kettle. The higher it climbs, the faster my heart pumps. I force myself not to look down, but fix my gaze above, on the sky. But it won't be long before the people who are praying in the mosque and on the streets will look up—the rug will need to go faster. Wrapping my trembling fingers around the carpet strings, I brace myself and pull the fringe straight up. The rug bolts toward the clouds.

I cry out at the suddenness of it and let go, falling back onto Rasheed. The rug slows down to its natural pace as he pushes me back up. Rasheed stares over the edge, his eyes widening.

"Praise Allah, it's the most amazing thing I've ever seen."

I cautiously peer over the carpet and gasp. We're even higher than I imagined. The people below look like tiny mustard seeds, scattered over the city. The great trees are strange little shrubs and sticks, and the buildings look like a baby's wooden blocks. The Tigris River is a shining silver snake in the sun. We can see the entire circular wall around the city, and all the gates at once. And there's the great dome!

When a bird flies beneath us, Rasheed laughs. "I've had dreams that I could fly like a bird."

I take hold of the fringe. "Now you can." Guiding the rug forward, I slowly put more pressure on the strings, and the carpet picks up speed. The wind swirls past us and pushes my scarf back from my face. Soon we're flying faster than a horse can gallop. I look behind me at Rasheed and smile; his arms are in the air.

"It's like my dream," he says, "but a thousand times better. I never thought—" He gazes at the tiny Palace of the Crown in the distance. "Marjana, today is the greatest day I've ever known."

His grin and the warmth of his words give me even more joy than the rush of wind on my face and the beauty of the city below us. I laugh. "But I better take us back now—Cook will be calling you for dinner soon. We'll have a lot of explaining to do if she can't find you anywhere!"

I steer the carpet around and swoop through the air, soaring up and down and swerving back and forth like a fish in the river, until we arrive where we started, hovering high above our street. I push the fringe downward and we descend. Most people have gone home for their evening meals and no one sees us sink between the buildings and glide through the open window. The house is filled with the aroma of stewed meat, and the magic lamp gives off a homey glow. Its flame flickers as we sweep into the room.

"Close, Sesame."

The rug lands softly on the floor exactly where it used to be. Everything is quiet and still. For several moments,

Rasheed and I sit silently staring at each other. It's almost as if it never happened and the carpet never moved, as if we never were flying high above Baghdad only moments ago. But it's true. The magic is real.

Rasheed reaches out his hand and squeezes mine. The look on his face—so trusting and kind—reminds me of Saja's. It's the look of a friend.

"Thank you, Marjana."

20

Leila doesn't sleep late like Mistress. Before the rooster's crow the next morning, when it's barely light outside, I hear her working in the garden. As soon as I put on my qamis and sirwal, I hear the woman whistling to herself. Leila's presence is like the comfort of a soft pillow or a soothing drink. I need to get going early, but instead of slipping out the shutter screen, I find myself walking out the back door to the garden.

"As-salaam alaykum, Marjana! Poor Cook; she must be burdened with too much work and needs help tidying the garden—I've found almost as many rotted melons as ripe." Leila shakes her head. She's already filled two large basketfuls of fruit and vegetables.

I don't have the heart to tell her that Cook is just too lazy to keep the garden nice. I drop to my knees beside her and start pulling weeds.

"Oh, thank you, dear. I've been hoping for a chance to talk with you. Are you all right?" She pats my knee.

I stare at the dirt and nod, unable to speak. Sometimes I can hide it or make it go away for a time, but I'm not all right. I have a full heart that aches to be released.

"Your brother told me what happened to his poor little friend Badi, Saja's brother. I'm sorry to hear of her loss. This must be hard for you, too, with Saja so distressed. I knew when I saw you two together what soul sisters you could be."

At the words *soul sisters*, the pent-up rivers I've worked hard to contain come bursting out with no warning. The wall I built around my heart is finally crumbling. The dam bursts, and water rises to my eyes.

"Saja hates me." Tears fall to the dirt.

Leila's soft words are a soothing balm on a raw wound. "Sometimes love is so strong it makes us weak, but if we embrace it, love holds us up and strengthens us." She takes my chin in her hand. "Saja doesn't hate you."

"How do you know?"

"I went to see her at the bathhouse yesterday. She said she'll try to come early—" Leila glances over her shoulder at the sound of footsteps.

Saja stands near the garden wall, her eyes red, her qamis rumpled.

I draw in my breath. Stumbling to my feet, I hurry to the wall. I can't get there fast enough.

Saja sinks into my arms like a wilted flower and weeps into my shoulder. "I'm sorry I gave you the pear seed, Marjana. I didn't mean it."

"You were in pain, Saja. I'm sorry I left you and Badi that night. I didn't know—"

"No, it's not your fault." Saja shakes her head. "Those words—I shouldn't have said them. I didn't know who to be angry at."

"I know. It's all right. That's how I felt when my mother died. I understand."

"It's *so hard*, Marjana. I feel like I can't go on; I don't know how. I'm not brave like you." She sighs. "I'm so . . . empty."

I shake my head. "No, you're not empty." The depth in Saja's eyes seems to go on and on like the countless layers holding up the world in Rasheed's story. I squeeze her hand. "There's a universe inside you."

Saja blinks, smiling through her tears. She draws me close, and I let her. *Soul sister.*

"It was so hard to be alone and think of Badi." Saja sniffs and wipes her nose. "I felt the lowest on the morning Jamal brought me your cracked cardamom in the courtyard a couple days ago. Instead of feeling better like I thought I would after giving you the pear seed, I felt worse. I needed a friend. I knew what happened to Badi wasn't your fault, but at the time, it felt better to have someone to blame. Your idea of letting Badi meet

Jamal wasn't what caused the problem. In fact, that day you offered to help me, I hoped I'd found a friend."

"I'm glad you didn't give up on me."

"Even when I was angry, I still thought of you. I wondered how you were. Every time I heard a lute play, or smelled jasmine—it seemed almost everything made me think of you. Especially when I heard the news." Saja's brow wrinkles. "Some of the women who came to the bathhouse yesterday said your master was dying of a choleric fever. I was so afraid you might get sick, too—"

"Shh!" I raise a finger to my lips and glance around the corner of the house. If anyone hears the truth, everything could come crashing down. "He's dead, but not from choleric—Master was killed. You can't say a word about it."

"Why? Who did it?" Saja's eyes grow wide.

I need to get started on my plan and head across town while it's still early, but the idea of leaving Saja after finally getting her back is crushing. "Come with me on an errand, and I'll tell you."

"Where are you going?"

"To a cobbler that Cook told me about on the far side of town."

"It's too early—shops aren't open yet. And why don't you just go to the cobbler down the street?"

"That's part of what I need to tell you about."

"I wish I could go with you, but I have to get back. I can walk with you as far as the bathhouse, but I can't go across town."

"All right. But you won't believe what's been happening around here." By the time we get to the bathhouse, I've told Saja the whole story, and her mouth hangs open. She clutches my hand so tightly, it feels like she might twist it off.

"A magic carpet? And a treasure cave?"

"Shh!"

"The Forty Thieves?"

"Shhhh!"

"And your master—ew!"

"Saja!" I take hold of her arm. "You must keep this to

yourself. Everyone's lives are at stake. If anyone suspects that Master was murdered, the entire household would be in danger."

Saja nods soberly. "But . . . what about your plan—won't the cobbler find out?"

"Don't worry about that. I thought of everything."

"Look." Saja points to a notice nailed to the bathhouse door. "The master of the baths read it to us this morning. There's one on the men's bathhouse, too, and all the cafés and inns. It says a private citizen has offered a reward through the magistrate to anyone giving information about the captain of the Forty Thieves that leads to his capture, whether he's dead or living! Ali Baba did this, didn't he?"

I nod. I can't picture the devil-man being thrown into a prison cell. "I counseled Ali Baba to offer some of his treasure money as a reward. Hopefully someone will find the captain before he finds us." It's unbearable to think of him when I'm so happy to have Saja back.

"It will be all right." She glances over her shoulder at

the bathhouse and sighs. "I'd better get back before I get in trouble."

"I'll see you as soon as I can."

"Marjana?"

"Yes?"

"Be careful!"

When Saja disappears into the steam, I turn and head toward northwest toward the Sham gate. I hurry through the narrow, mazelike streets, under the over-hanging balconies. Around the eastern horizon, the sky wears a scarf of gold and crimson threads. Although the morning birds are in full chorus, Baghdad is still drowsy. Most shop owners are just rising from their mats, but Mustaphas, a cobbler near the gate, is known for opening his shop at the break of dawn.

The sprightly old man perches behind the stall in front of his shop under the vaulted arcade, a piece of leather in his hands. His long white hair curls up around his turban, and his beard almost touches his sash.

"As-salaam alaykum!" he exclaims when he sees me.

"Early customers are the best customers. What can I do for you?"

"Wa alaykum as-salaam." I press one of Ali Baba's gold pieces into his withered palm and whisper in his ear, "Gather your needles and thread. I have a job for you in exchange for the gold that rests in your hand and another when the task is finished."

The cobbler smiles a toothless grin and closes his fingers around the gold. "No need to ask me twice!"

"I'll guide you, but you must wear this around your eyes." I pull a handkerchief from my sash.

"What—"

"No questions, or there is no bargain." I blindfold Mustaphas and silently lead him through the backstreets of Baghdad to Master's house. We don't meet a single person on the way.

Once inside, I take him to the dark room where the body lies and untie the handkerchief. The man's eyes boggle as he watches me unfold the bundles that hold Master's quartered body.

My fingers tremble. A cold stone falls into the pit of my stomach. Bile climbs to my throat, but I don't turn away. "You must sew these quarters together as I watch you work."

The old man takes a step backward and his eyes grow round as pan bread. But when I show him the gold dinar again, he sighs and solemnly begins to thread his needle and dutifully performs his gruesome task in silence. Though my knees turn weak, I am determined to see the job finished, if only to be able to tell Rasheed that I did it.

When the work's completed, the bare thread of the tiny stitches on Master's skin is the only evidence of his grisly murder. I wince when I remember the fortune-teller's words to Master: *Alas, you will die threadbare.* He had even foreseen this! Surely Abu-Zayed must know more than he revealed.

I give the cobbler his dinar, cover his eyes, and lead him back to his shop by way of the side streets. As far as I can tell, no one sees us. I thank Mustaphas, who marvels at his two gold coins, and I return home by the usual route. The hard part's done—soon it will all be over.

But the devil-man still haunts me. Surely when he realizes that someone else knows the secret of the treasure cave, he'll come looking for the person who removed Master's body. I shiver. *If he finds Ali Baba, will he do the same thing to him?*

21

I'm glad to finally have it all over and done with. Earlier this afternoon, Ali Baba prepared a grand funeral for Master. Yet again, it's just as Abu-Zayed predicted: *In the end, any dignity you have left, you will owe to the charity of your brother.* I joined Mistress and Leila in leading the crowd of hired mourning women through the streets as a band played. Master's sewn-up body was paraded through Baghdad to the graveyard, and no one had been the wiser as to his true cause of death.

I smile beneath my veil as I walk home from the bazaar that evening with my bundles. Rasheed will laugh when I tell him about the monkey who mimicked its owner at the fruit seller's stall. Ali Baba's son has proved every one of my assumptions wrong. He's far from a sour, lazy young man. In fact, he and his father are using the gold to turn Master's shop into a religious school. The madrasa will have the finest teachers and provide room and board for the students, even if they're poor. Because the building is next door to the house, Ali Baba can easily help Rasheed walk there to attend classes himself. They also bought the building next to the shop to give to the mosque. The imam promises to help Rasheed and Ali Baba turn it into a shelter for homeless street children.

Leila brings a cheery aura to the home, which comforts Mistress and softens her attitude toward us. Their conversation and laughter carry throughout the house and warm my heart in a way I haven't felt since Mother was with us.

Ali Baba's family is accustomed to eating together. I have never heard of such a thing. Men and women live in separate worlds, but Ali Baba and Leila see things differently than most people, perhaps even other Sufis.

When I'd shown my surprise at serving them together, Ali Baba said, "I know it seems unusual, but Leila and I see no reason to stay apart unless we have guests who might be offended. It's true we all find ourselves in different forms here on earth, but ultimately there is no male or female, only Being."

Only Being. Such beautiful words. I squeeze my bundles to my chest and smile as I walk. But when I reach the house, all pleasant thoughts fly from my head. Someone hurries away from the steps and disappears around the street corner. And there, on the front door, someone has drawn a small mark with a piece of chalk. It's barely noticeable, really. A chalk mark is hardly a thing to invite panic. Perhaps it's merely a game. But my heart races like a darabukka drum. Maybe the robbers discovered where Ali Baba lives. If one of them made the mark and means to return with the rest of the thieves . . .

I drop my baskets and fumble over the ground,

searching for a chalky stone. Scurrying up and down the street, I draw similar marks on all the houses nearby. Now Ali Baba's door looks exactly like the rest. I take a deep breath and release it. Gathering my bundles, I go inside and almost shout out the news, but at the last moment, I hold my tongue. Alarming the household will only make things worse—especially if Mistress finds out. No, it's best to keep it to myself. Ali Baba trusts me to be in charge, and I don't want him to doubt his decision. But the anxiety on my face doesn't escape Rasheed's notice.

"Marjana, are you all right?"

My nerves are lute strings that are wound too tightly. I nod. It feels as if the slightest strain might snap me in two. That evening as we listen to his stories after dinner, I wish I could relax and let Rasheed's wondrous tales take hold of my imagination. The way he spins such wild adventures as "The Clever Princess and the Bold Thief Who Loved Her" make my heart beat faster than Jamal can play his drum. But instead of letting it lift my spirits,

I can't stop thinking about the chalk mark on the door.

The next morning, Mistress bids me prepare a basket of fresh fruit to take with us to the bathhouse. I hurry outside to pick some figs, anxious to see Saja again. When I glance at the front of the house, my heart leaps to my throat. Another chalk mark has been scrawled on the door, this time in red. I throw down the basket and run to find a red stone. Again, I mark the houses on either side, up and down the street.

"What's wrong, dear?" Leila asks as we collect the things we'll take to the baths.

"Nothing." I force myself to smile. "I'm just not feeling well today, but going to the bathhouse will help."

As soon as we arrive, I find Saja kneeling over a reclining woman, applying henna to her hair. When she sees me, she rinses her hands in a bowl of water and runs over to kiss both my cheeks. Her eyes are red.

I smooth back her tangled hair from her face. "Are you all right?"

Saja shakes her head. "I think of Badi all the time. It's

so hard." She wipes her eyes. "But having you helps." She squeezes my hand.

I glance at the naked woman lying facedown on the warm bath tiles.

"Don't mind her," Saja whispers. "I think she's asleep." The woman snores, as if to confirm it. Saja takes hold of my shoulders. "There's something I have to tell you!"

"What's wrong?"

She hesitates, wringing her hands. Her finger tips are stained orange from henna. "Some of the bathhouse boys say Red Beard is back and he's planning another battle. One of the boys saw Red Beard's man near Ali Baba's house. He must be planning a battle in your neighborhood, Marjana. I'm worried about you. And what if he has the gangs break into Rasheed's new madrasa?"

"What?" I go limp. My head's spinning. The marks on the wall must have something to do with Red Beard's street gangs. "Are they sure it was Red Beard's man? I thought—"

"Well, none of the boys knows for sure what's going

on, but if it's true, Rasheed's dream for a school will be ruined, and you'll all be in danger." A line of worry appears across Saja's forehead.

The bath patron stirs and lifts herself up on her elbows, glaring at Saja through muddy clumps of hair.

"Oh," Saja says. "I have to go." She lets her hand slide from mine and sighs. "Be on your guard, Marjana."

— ◈ —

When no marks appear the following morning, I breathe a sigh of relief. Perhaps it's all a mistake and nothing will come of it. The bath boys haven't been summoned to the dumping grounds, and no one has actually seen Red Beard return. Maybe it was just a rumor, and the marks are child's play, that's all.

I let myself relax a little. After evening meal, Cook goes to bed early. When the dishes are gathered and the food cleared away, I sit alone in my room, near the window, listening to the sound of Ali Baba laughing with his wife and son in the other room. Deep inside, I ache to have what they have. It's what I wish for every time

I dream of Umi—a family, people who love and need me.

I reach for my lute. My fingers glide over the curves of the smooth wood and rest on the familiar strings. Rasheed's deep voice makes me pause.

"Now, Jamal, do you remember where we left off last time?" He's telling another tale about Scheherazade, a queen whose husband planned to execute her. Scheherazade told the king an exciting story every evening, but she always withheld the ending. The captivated king would spare her life another day in order to hear the rest of the tale. By continuing her stories, Scheherazade saved her life and the lives of countless other wives who the wicked king had planned to marry and murder.

"Yes!" pipes Jamal. "Scheherazade was telling the tale of Sinbad's third voyage! He set sail from Basra and was marooned on an island where he was captured by a monster with eyes like coals of fire and large teeth like boar's tusks!"

"Ah, yes," Rasheed says. "That's right. Well, you'll never guess what happens next!"

I walk quietly through the hall and stand near the door, listening as Rasheed resumes the tale he started the night before.

"But please don't stop at the most exciting part this time, Rasheed!" Jamal begs.

I try stifling the laugh rising in my throat, but I can't keep the giggle from escaping.

Rasheed pauses. "We haven't even got to the funny part yet, Marjana," he says, starting to laugh, himself.

I poke my head around the doorway.

Leila motions me into the room and fluffs the pillows beside her. "Come join us!" Jamal kneels in front of Rasheed, transfixed, like a heathen worshiping a god.

I settle myself on the comfortable cushions next to Mistress and Leila. Ali Baba's probably sitting outside the front door, resting in the coolness, as is his habit in the evenings.

Just when I start losing myself in the excitement of Rasheed's story, Ali Baba walks into the room. He clears his throat, and Rasheed stops talking.

"I've invited a guest to stay the night—an oil merchant who was passing by and stopped to talk to me. He hasn't the money for an inn, and he needs a place to stay. Surely, we remember what it's like to be poor, so please welcome my guest."

The women and I pull our scarves over our faces as the oil merchant follows Ali Baba into the room.

"As-salaam alaykum," everyone murmurs as the women retire to the harem.

"Marjana," Ali Baba says, "please see to my friend's needs. He's had a long journey."

The man is tall and slender, with a dark beard and high cheekbones. He wears a patch over one eye, and a scar runs across his right cheek. His clothes don't appear to be from around here, and he's carrying a few small bundles.

I bow and take his belongings to a chamber upstairs, disappointed that I'll miss the story Rasheed's telling. While Ali Baba visits with the merchant, I ready the man's room and prepare a broth for him as I strain to listen to Rasheed's voice.

He soon finishes his storytelling, and Jamal begs him to tell the ending, but Rasheed only laughs and says he'll have to wait until next time. I smile to myself and slip my scarf off while I cook. Rasheed sends Jamal to bed. Before long, the house turns completely quiet, but for the sound of the spoon scraping the pot.

As I dip the ladle into the soup, my lamp flickers and goes out. That's the last oil I have in the house. If only I had my own magic lamp! I sigh, thinking of the oil merchant upstairs in his room. Surely he has jars of oil that were unloaded in the back courtyard. He won't miss just a little, in order to get his own supper made.

I take a kettle and walk quietly out to the backyard. The large leather oil jugs stand near the stables. The merchant's chamber is nearby, so I tiptoe across the yard and pull on the lid of the first container.

As I lift it, a low voice whispers from the jar, "Is it time?"

22

I almost drop the lid when I hear the voice coming from the huge oil jar. A scream of terror leaps to my throat, but I swallow it just in time. *Are jinn stuck inside the jars?* But then the awful truth flies to my mind a moment later— the robbers!

Fear courses through my body. The captain found us and is pretending to be the traveling merchant. Ali Baba, Leila, Rasheed, Mistress, and little Jamal are all sleeping in the house with a murderer. The men are awaiting the devil-man's command to attack and kill them all! My first impulse is to run and wake the household, but I rein in my fears and think fast. Causing a commotion would put everyone in danger, and we would be outnumbered and overpowered. My knees go weak.

I take a breath to calm myself, swallow, and wet my lips. Trying to make my voice sound deep like a man's, I whisper back, "It's not yet time, but presently." My whole body quivers—a ruthless thief with a knife in his hand is curled up inside each jar. I force myself to continue walking alongside all the jars, lifting each lid just a crack and repeating this answer as I pass. Finally, I come to the last jar, which contains oil the devil-man used to fool Ali Baba into believing he was a merchant. I need to do something quickly. If only I could get help. A breeze blows in from the marketplace, curls around me, and sweeps back toward the empty bazaar.

Abu-Zayed, the fortune-teller! He'll know what to do because he already knows what will happen! I remember the smirk on his face before he gave Master his fortune, and a shiver runs down my spine. A man who consorts with harmful jinn is the last person I should be asking for help. May Allah forgive me for seeking him out, but I must save Ali Baba's family. I fly down the road leading to the marketplace. The devil-man might give his men the signal to attack while I'm gone if I don't hurry. My hair whips around my face, stinging my eyes, and my long qamis gets twisted in my legs as I run.

Some men walking down the dark street stop and stare at me tearing down the road, my unpinned hair flying out behind me. They point and shout at me, but I don't care. I have to find Abu-Zayed. He'll know what to do.

I finally reach the market and find him in his usual spot lying against the stall, and I shake his frail frame. "Wake up! Abu-Zayed, I need your help!"

His eyes open, and he smiles slowly, as if he's been expecting me. "Is it time?" he asks calmly.

"Please come help me!" I pull the old man to his feet.

"Of course. I have been waiting years for this moment." Abu-Zayed takes hold of my arm and runs along with me.

"What should I do?" I gasp. "They're waiting to kill us! What do I do?"

Abu-Zayed already seems to know who I'm talking about. "You must be brave."

"But what should I *do*?"

"You must be strong."

"But how?" I cry, angry at the man for staying so calm. "I can't wake the household or the men will jump out and kill us all. And I can't wake anyone in the neighborhood. There's a band of ruthless killers in the courtyard just waiting to swarm—our neighbors wouldn't stand a chance!"

I go faster as we approach the house. "If we fetch the magistrate or the commander of the army, it might take too long."

We pause at the street corner. Abu-Zayed remains quiet.

I throw my hands up, exasperated. "Our only chance is if I stop them before they make a move." There doesn't seem to be any other way. I try to swallow the lump forming in my throat. Abu-Zayed doesn't answer but continues alongside me as we hurry back to the house. Nothing had changed; all is quiet. I glance around the courtyard, thinking fast. The oil? I could heat it to boiling and pour it into each jar, killing the thieves inside. Foolishness. This isn't one of Rasheed's wild stories—this is real. It would take a whole jar of oil for each man, and the screaming of the first would wake the rest. I shiver in horror.

Finally, Abu-Zayed speaks. "You were right when you said at the beginning that *waking* people is not the answer."

"Yes," I say impatiently. "But what *is* the an—"

The sleeping potion. My blood pumps faster as the idea takes shape. Kadir and Kadira gave me the sleeping potion for Master, which is just sitting on a shelf inside since Master didn't really need it. *One drop will ease the pain of dying,* they said, *and bring days of deep, peaceful sleep, almost like death itself.*

I lead Abu-Zayed to the kitchen and find the sleeping potion, my breath coming fast. Taking some loaves of pan bread, I break them into thirty-nine pieces and carefully pour the potion onto them—one drop for each piece, to put the murderers to sleep until we can fetch the magistrate. I give Abu-Zayed half the bread, and we carry the baskets to the courtyard. I stop and stare at the thirty-nine jars and glance at Abu-Zayed. He gazes back at me, his eyes narrowing as he waits for me to continue.

What if they suspect something and rise from their jars?

I grip the basket of bread. Umi would want me to protect Jamal. And what about Ali Baba, Leila, and Rasheed? Their kindness is worth more than gold.

I take a deep breath. Then, with all the courage I can muster, I nod to Abu-Zayed, and we step toward the first jars. As I lift the lid a crack in the darkness, I'm afraid my trembling fingers will drop it, exposing me to the thief inside and alerting the others. I swallow hard and steady my grip on the lid. The poisoned flat bread is like a stone in my hand, but I force myself to slip it through the crack. The sound of movement inside the jar almost makes me bolt, but the thief is merely trying to retrieve the bread. Hoping my voice won't tremble, I say in a low tone, "Strengthen yourself—the time is near," and shut the lid.

I haven't realized how much I'm shaking until I try to breathe. My whole body convulses. Across the way, Abu-Zayed shuts a lid. He wears a strange look on his face—a mixture of grim satisfaction and . . . pleasure. The hairs on my arm stand on end as he grins and steps to the next one.

I stare at my long row of oil jars and gulp back a moan. But I step forward and crack open the next lid. "Strengthen yourself—the time is near." I do it again and again, sliding in the bread and listening to the thief find it. Each time, my stomach clenches as I imagine the thief bounding out of the jar and swiping off my head. Finally, all the bread is gone; a piece is in each jar.

Pulse throbbing, I rush with Abu-Zayed back to the kitchen where the devil-man's supper still sits where I left it, half-prepared. We put out the fire and wait breathlessly in the dark near the window to see what will happen. The devil-man can't come before the potion takes effect, or we'll all still be in danger. I picture the thieves inside the jars, eating their bread and slipping into a deep sleep.

In about a quarter of an hour, the shutters of the captain's chamber window creak open, and a handful of pebbles rain down against the jars. When the thieves don't respond to his signal, the captain climbs down into the yard.

His dark silhouette in the moonlight brings back memories of the kidnapping, when he stared at me with his face in shadow, the serpent on his chest ready to strike. I remember the feel of the ropes cutting into my wrists and the taste of fear in my mouth. Now it seems like it's happening all over again.

The captain slides his scimitar from its sheath and walks silently through the courtyard. He whispers over the jars, "Are you asleep? Arise!"

Hearing no response, he cuts open a leather jar.

The limp hand of one of his sleeping companions slides out and slaps the ground. The devil-man stands for a moment, staring at the lifeless body before walking down the long row of jars. He must think the men are all dead. He stops. His body straightens, and he jerks around with a sudden forceful movement.

I hold my breath. Will he leave or come after us on his own?

Abu-Zayed stirs beside me. "Captain!" The fortune-teller's calm voice floats over the courtyard. I cover my mouth so the cry won't escape. He must be truly mad.

The devil-man steps forward into the moonlight. I duck down farther into the shadows and peek out between the crack and the door.

The old fortune-teller steps from the kitchen doorway. I blink at him in disbelief from my hiding place.

The devil-man's face turns ashen, as if he's seen a ghoul. His merchant eye patch and scar are gone. The captain wears gold and silver necklaces over his bare chest, and his turban gleams white. "Abu-Zayed," he murmurs. "You live." He takes a few paces toward the old man. "Have you missed your treasure cave, or do you prefer to make your living telling fortunes?" The devil-man walks even closer to Abu-Zayed and gestures toward the jars. "So you finally got your revenge after all these years. But it is a shame you could not predict your own fate. *I* predict you will not leave here alive when I kill you *this* time."

The devil-man draws his sword and, in one quick movement, strikes the old man in the side. Abu-Zayed falls to his knees.

I stifle a cry and drop to the kitchen floor.

Abu-Zayed clutches the wound and slumps forward, a terrible laugh coming from deep within his throat. "Yes, revenge. I have waited a long time for this. I came to tell you your fortune." He coughs in pain.

The captain laughs. "Well, you'd better hurry and tell me, before you die."

Abu-Zayed struggles to speak. "It is this: The very treasure you've stolen from me and hoarded all these years will be given away freely."

The devil-man frowns.

"There is more." Abu-Zayed coughs. "You have lived by the sword as someone you were not. Soon you shall die by the sword of one who is not what they were. I only wish I could be here to see it."

With that, the old man sinks to the ground.

The devil-man stands over him for a moment, looking proud and triumphant like a stone god. Finally, he slides his sword into its sheath and makes his escape through the garden door.

CHAPTER

23

I'm jolted out of my shock by the sound of Ali Baba calling my name from the house. It's still dark; the sun has yet to rise. I push myself from the cold ground where I've crawled and collapsed at the crumpled form of poor Abu-Zayed. My limbs are stiff, frozen. Like a person in a trance, I walk to the kitchen, where Ali Baba stands scratching his head in confusion.

"What's happening?" he asks, bewildered. "I thought I heard a commotion. It turns out my guest crept away in the night! What kind of merchant travels in the dark?" He shrugs his thin shoulders and shakes his head.

"Oh, Ali Baba, he was no more a merchant than I

am!" I make Ali Baba sit down and, in a trembling voice, tell him what happened. His eyes widen as he listens to the story.

When I finish, he holds out his arms to me. "Praise to Allah!" he cries. "I owe my life and my family's lives to you."

I breathe in the warm smell of soap and hookah smoke that linger in his clothes and wonder if this is what it feels like to be hugged by a father.

Ali Baba clasps his hands together and clears his throat as if he has something important to say. "After my brother's funeral, his property was officially given over to me. Now I can finally declare you and your brother legally free, Marjana. It is certainly the least I can do."

I blink in surprise, not knowing what to say. "But Jamal and I don't have anywhere to go and no connections to find employment. . . ." I can't bear to leave now. Jamal, Saja, and Ali Baba's family are the only ones in the world who mean anything to me.

"I was hoping that instead of looking for work elsewhere, you and Jamal could work and live here as family servants—we would pay you very well to be sure." Ali Baba smiles. "We would miss you both if you were to leave."

The hollowness inside doesn't feel so hollow anymore. Being wanted feels good and warm and solid. Almost like it must feel to have a real home. Almost.

Ali Baba wakes Rasheed and tells him the story, asking him to keep the servants indoors and to recite the Qur'an over Abu-Zayed's body. Then Ali Baba and I hurry to the magistrate, who summons his men to bind the sleeping thieves and take them away. Ali Baba and I conduct proper burial rights for the dead man. Even though he was a fortune-teller, Ali Baba insists we bathe and enshroud him before praying, turning his head toward Mecca, and finally burying him.

That evening, after prayers, I slip away to my room, exhausted. The strength I'd gathered to face the danger has finally dissolved. Although I know I've done the right thing, my ribs ache from the heaviness of my heart. I fall on my mat and weep until sleep has mercy on me and carries me away.

— ◈ —

Weeks pass with no further signs of the devil-man, though I look for him everywhere. The thieves have all woken up in their prison cells, but not one has said a word in betrayal of their captain to the magistrate. I decide that the devil-man's fate must have come upon him just as the fortune-teller predicted. I still have moments of nagging worry, but Abu-Zayed had never been wrong before, and I have no reason to doubt his words. I finally allow myself to breathe easier and begin settling back into ordinary life.

Although Saja says Red Beard has returned to the dumping grounds and the street battles have resumed, all is quiet in Ali Baba's neighborhood. Jamal and I spend our evenings listening to Rasheed's adventure tales of jinn and giants, pirates and kings. Often, when Rasheed finishes his story, he asks us to accompany him on our instruments as he plays the ney.

Since that night I ran to fetch Abu-Zayed without my scarf, I never wear it around the house anymore. I've grown comfortable with Ali Baba and his family seeing my unveiled eyes when I speak to them. My smile always seems to nudge one to the lips of Ali Baba and Leila. My frown causes little lines to crinkle on Rasheed's forehead, and when I grimace, it pulls a laugh from deep within his throat. So many of my feelings have been hidden by my scarf. Sharing them with Ali Baba's family soon feels as natural as breathing.

One morning, I'm trimming the rose vines near the windows at the front of the house, when something small and hard hits me on the head.

"Ow!" I glance around to see who threw the pebble.

A boy with dark curly hair and no turban pokes his head out from behind a cypress tree. *Stinger!* He checks to see that the street is clear, then runs up to the house. He doesn't seem to recognize me. He bows politely, despite the fact he's just hit me with a stone. "Hey you—girl! I have to ask you a question. Is this where Ali Baba lives?" He scratches his dirty chin with the wildcat's fang.

I frown at him. So it's true about Red Beard's plan! I slam my knife, which I'm using to cut the roses, against the sill. "You tell Red Beard and his gangs that they'd better stay away from Ali Baba's madrasa, or I'll . . . I'll . . ." I can't think what to say next.

Stinger's eyes grow wide in surprise. "How do you know about Red Beard?"

"I—" I don't know what to say. I pick the knife up again and stick the point into the sill.

He squints at my eyes, then stares at the dagger. His mouth falls open. He searches my face. "Khubz?" He stumbles backward from the shock.

"Yes, it's me," I whisper. "I was just trying to keep an eye on my little brother that night. That's not important right now—tell me what Red Beard's planning to do!"

Stinger shakes his head, as if trying to wake from a dream. "But . . . you're a girl."

I glare at him.

He eyes my fingers tightening around the dagger. "A girl with a knife," he adds.

"Is Red Beard planning a battle for Ali Baba's property or not?"

"Yes!" Stinger spits a wad of his black chewing leaves into the dirt. "He wants the bathies to break in tonight and take everything, just like the plan to raid the merchant's on Umar Hill. We're supposed to battle them, but they'll get the loot anyway."

"Oh no!"

"Yep, Red Beard says the winnings will be tremendous. It will be the biggest, bloodiest gang battle in the history of Baghdad."

I shudder. How will we be able to defend ourselves?

"He says scribes will write about it in the city's history accounts."

"But—"

"And that if I do this right, I'll become one of his men."

"Stinger—"

"But I won't."

"What?"

"We won't let them take a thing."

My mouth drops open.

"Our gang knows Ali Baba, and we're going to fight for his building."

I almost fall into the rosebushes. "How do you know Ali Baba?"

"He's come to the mosque on our street almost every morning for years. He learned all our names and always invites us in to pray. At first, none of us did, but lately, he's brought a big basket of food and gives us a morning meal every day, so now most of us go. And we heard he's building a madrasa and a shelter for street kids." Stinger glances at the large house and adjoining building. "I guess he had some good fortune and wants to share it with us."

I'm speechless.

Stinger stands up straighter. "He's a good man. It

doesn't seem fair to us that Red Beard wants to take everything Ali Baba has when he actually uses his wealth to help so many people. We can't let the bathies and Red Beard destroy his building."

"You're absolutely right." I cut the thorns off a yellow rose and smile as I hand the flower to Stinger. "We definitely can't let that happen."

24

The night presses against the mango-colored sun till its juices trickle out across the horizon. From our window, Jamal and I watch for Saja. Soon her familiar silhouette appears against the sunset, and I reach through the window and help her over the ledge.

Inside, Saja greets me with a kiss on both cheeks. "I got here as soon as I could." When she notices Jamal, Saja stares sadly at him for a moment. I know she's missing her own brother. Then Saja smiles at him and kisses his cheeks, too. Though he screws up his eyes as if the kisses bring him pain, he doesn't squirm away.

"I'm glad you came," I tell her. "Stinger says we can help

by holding off the gang if they get here early before his gang arrives. He says it will be a small group—just the bathhouse boys—Red Beard won't even show up, but we have to make sure they're stopped before they ruin Ali Baba."

"Eww!" Saja groans, pinching her nose. "What's that stench?"

"That's the smell of our secret weapons." I nod to the corner where I placed the baskets of rotten produce Leila picked from the garden.

"Secret weapons!" Jamal's eyes light up.

"Good thing Cook is so lazy." I take hold of his chin and squish his cheeks so his lips pucker. "Now you have to follow my orders, understand?" I try forcing him to look me in the eye, but his gaze keeps straying to the secret weapons.

"We don't want Ali Baba and his family to even know about this or worry about us. We can help them just like they've helped us. So, go listen to Rasheed's story, Jamal, but after everyone goes to bed, meet us on the roof of his madrasa, next door. Just climb the tree. We'll be waiting for you there. With these!" I lift the lid of one of the baskets, and Saja and Jamal both moan at the smell of the rotten fruit and vegetables. When Jamal leaves, Saja and I slip on our boy clothes in preparation for the battle and sit near the window in the falling dark. The thought of spoiling Red Beard's plan and helping Ali Baba, Leila, and Rasheed gives me a thrill and makes me feel more alive.

My dreams about Umi coming back will never come true, but there are things I never dreamed of—having a new kind of family—that seem to be within my reach. I finally know what it is I really want. And I'm willing to fight for it.

Saja and I hurry to put on our turbans. She hands the smelly baskets out the window to me, and I carry them over to the bushes near the madrasa. We run to the back courtyard to get a rope from the stable. I carry it around my neck as I climb the ancient cypress tree's gnarled branches that cling to the side of the building.

When I step to the roof, I stand there, gazing out at the

city. Baghdad twinkles like firebugs in the dusky evening. Over the rooftops, the world spreads out before me and I'm at the center of it. Its circling rim meets the edge of the heavens above me. The sight takes my breath away. Being at the center of such a vast space makes me feel both small and enormous at the same time.

The apothecary shop, the market, the bathhouse, the mosque, and even Umar Hill are in view. In the distance, a bit of the dumping grounds and the beautiful Taj Palace are visible as well. At that moment, it feels as if the whole world belongs to me. The night air is like a tonic; I drink it in and let it fill up every part of my body.

"Marjana!" Saja shakes some branches of the tree to get my attention. "Throw down the end of the rope."

I let it drop, and Saja ties one of the baskets to the end. As I pull it up, the rope makes a scratching sound against the edge of the roof, and the basket bangs against the wall.

"Stop!" Saja whispers. "Someone's coming."

She jumps into the bushes to hide. I peer over the roof and try to keep the basket from moving as it hangs suspended, halfway up.

Cook stumbles around the corner and through the alleyway between the house and madrasa, clutching one of Master's wine jugs. Since Ali Baba and his family don't drink the wine left in Master's house, Cook had gotten into the habit of helping herself to a jug every once in a while after her work is done. She looks as if she's almost drained the one in her hand.

"Who's there?" Cook calls into the darkness.

I move slightly, and the basket thuds against the wall.

"Be you men or jinn?" Cook cries. Her voice slurs, and she looks as if she might tip over. She stands almost directly under the basket now. If she looks up, she'll surely see it, hanging like a magical gift in the sky. A rustling in the bushes startles her.

The noise startles me, too. I lose my grip on the rope for a moment, and the basket tips. A very soft, very rotten carrot falls onto Cook's head.

She squeals and swats at it. The limp carrot slips down her front and slaps against her jug of wine before landing on the ground. Cook gasps. "'Twas the Devil's hand! He wants the evil drink!" She moans and throws the bottle into the bushes. "I'll never drink again! In the name of Allah, I swear I'll never touch another drop!" She turns and flees the alleyway as a loud snort issues from the bushes and the jug of wine flies back out.

Saja emerges from the bush rubbing her head, her turban lopsided. "Seems whenever I'm with you, I get hit by flying objects and end up in the bushes!" she grumbles.

I try not to laugh as Saja ties the other basket to the rope. After I pull it over the ledge, Saja struggles up the tree, and I help her onto the roof. Short of breath, we lie down to rest and stare up at the stars to wait for Stinger's gang or the bathhouse boys to arrive. Everything is quiet.

Saja points to the brightest star, glowing like an

ember below the swollen moon. "Look how big that star is. Make a wish, Marjana."

I gaze at its light and whisper, "I wish to keep this, always."

"Keep what?"

"This moment. This freedom."

Saja whispers, "Marjana, what does it feel like to be free?"

"The freedom Ali Baba gave me?" I think for a moment. "Like someone gave me a knife to cut the ropes around my heart."

"I still think of that dream I had about being free and having my own shop. My own life." Saja sighs.

"I know it's very different to have real freedom. But Saja, in a way, you're freer than many people I know. Abu-Zayed had been enslaved by his treasure cave, just as the devil-man is now. Master was prisoner to his greed and his obsession with changing his fortune. Even me; I wouldn't let anyone in after Umi died, until you came along. My thoughts don't have a master. Neither do yours." I smile at the stars. "No matter what binds us on the outside, Saja, our hearts will always be free to do as they wish. Who can stop them?"

Saja gazes at the heavens, too. "No one?"

A shooting star streaks across the sky. Somewhere an angry angel hurled it at the nosy jinni. I imagine the jinni hurrying to a fortune-teller to share the news of some mortal's fate. I close my eyes and think of the vengeful Abu-Zayed.

Saja shivers as a breeze sweeps over the roof of the madrasa. "But no one can change their fate—slave or free." Her voice sounds small.

"Well, someone once told me that the threads of fate are our own, and we have the power to make them strong and beautiful." I sigh. "But sometimes I don't know if I have it in me."

Saja smiles. "Well, I know that you do. I will tell you what someone once told me: 'There's a universe inside you.'"

I laugh.

At that moment, the tree starts shaking. Saja lets out a little scream. Jamal's face appears over the edge. He hunches down on his hands and knees as soon as he crawls over the ledge and whispers, "They're coming!"

"Here!" I hand Jamal a basket of rotten fruit and vegetables and peek over the edge. A swarm of armed bathies run up the street, headed toward the madrasa.

"Where's Stinger's gang?" Saja cries.

"Don't worry," I whisper. "He'll be here. We'll hold them off until they come. Now, wait until the bathies start to break in. At my signal."

We all grab a weapon. Saja screws up her face at the smell, but wraps her fingers around a moldy melon. I choose an ancient head of lettuce.

The bathies' white qamis glow like bleached stones on the dark street. They're close enough for us to see their faces. Several carry lamps, and some have large clubs to break down the doors and shutters. The others brandish their weapons in case anyone tries to stop them. As soon as the boys raise their clubs to the door, I whisper, "Go!"

I aim at one of the clubbers and hurl my rotten lettuce right at his face. The blow is so unexpected that the boy drops his club and falls into the bathie behind him, who was just raising his arm to throw a stone.

A boy next to them gawks in confusion at his friends, struggling in the dirt.

Jamal gets another boy while his club is in mid-swing. He falls to the ground with mango smeared over his face.

The gang members glance around wildly at each other, trying to figure out what's happening.

Saja misses the boy she's aiming for, but manages to knock the stone from the hand of his companion. Jamal quickly pummels two rotten apples into the gang, knocking over three boys. By this time, the bathies have noticed the rotten smell—they wrinkle their noses and look around.

Then they look up.

When they see us, they scurry over the ground

looking for rocks to throw at their mysterious enemies on the roof.

I think quickly and aim my onion at another boy. When the onion hits his arm, he drops his lamp in the dirt, spilling the oil and snuffing it out. "Aim for the lamps!" I whisper.

"But they've found the tree!" Jamal points at some boys running into the alleyway.

"Keep them on the ground. Saja and I will work on the others!"

"They're already halfway up!" Jamal yells.

We can't keep going much longer. I aim at another lamp holder, but miss. I only have a few vegetables left.

"Marjana!" Saja gasps. "They're going to break the door down!"

I lean over the roof to look and get hit on the hand with a rock.

"Are you okay?" Saja screams.

I nod. "Just keep throwing!" My fingers turn numb; my wrist goes weak. Although the cut isn't deep, I won't be able to throw any more vegetables.

The roof shakes as the bathies' clubs hit the door of the madrasa. At that moment, a cry like a wildcat's pierces the night. A great shout rises up in answer.

Stinger!

Saja and I stand up. Stinger and his gang rush up the street like a dust storm, knocking over the bathies and blinding them in surprise. I cheer and run with Saja to help Jamal fight off the last of the boys who are climbing the tree.

It isn't long before the whole gang turns tail and runs like a herd of sheep bolting down the street. Saja, Jamal, and I clamber down from the roof to join Stinger and his gang as they whoop and laugh at the retreating bathies.

Shutters on nearby houses slide open, and doors crack as neighbors peek out to watch the bathhouse gang run away. I notice Ali Baba and his family peering out their windows in amazement. I almost wave in my excitement, but remember just in time that they have never met Khubz before. It might be best to keep it that way.

Stinger claps me on the back. He's tucked the yellow rose I gave him into his belt. "Nicely done, Khubz. Nicely done."

I slap him on the back, too. "Not so bad, yourself! A little late, but nicely done. For a boy."

Stinger laughs and then squints at Saja.

She's already blushing as she looks at Stinger.

He grins at her. "You've got a good throwing arm there . . . Lumpy."

Saja smiles and says, "You can call me Saja."

"Well, 'Lumpy' was all right, but I like 'Saja' better." He glances over the street. "We'd better get going before the neighbors come out." And before I can say 'Wa alaykum as-salaam,' Stinger flies like a wild bird with his flock of boys, down the street and out of sight.

Saja and I run around the house to the window. She helps me climb in. "I need to get back to the bathhouse, but I'll come see you tomorrow night. I have something to give you," she whispers. "And, Khubz?"

I lean out the window, my elbows on the sill. "What, Lumpy?"

"Thank you."

"For what? Getting you into bushes and having you help me throw stinky food?"

Saja smiles. "Thank you for twisting our fates together."

"I think it will be a beautiful thread." Our thoughts seem close enough to touch. "Strong and beautiful."

25

The next evening, I feel slightly guilty for frightening Cook the night before, so I help her prepare dinner with Jamal. We're making partridge with quince, and the kitchen is full of the aroma of fennel, onion, and saffron. As Jamal fetches the salt, I lower the bird into the simmering pot and Cook fetches more flour from the storeroom.

Ali Baba pokes his head into the kitchen. "We have a fine guest for dinner!"

"Who is this 'fine guest'?" Ever since the oil merchant turned out to be the captain of the robbers, I am leery of strangers.

"His name is Khoja Hoseyn, the gentleman who bought the shop across the street from the madrasa. He is a fine, dignified man. Very polite and pleasant. He had asked my son to dine, but Rasheed cannot attend alone, due to his weak legs. So, Rasheed has invited Khoja Hoseyn here, instead!"

I cross my arms over my chest and stare hard at Ali Baba. He is too trusting of strangers.

"He is an honest man, Marjana," Ali Baba says. "We are very fortunate to have him in our neighborhood. If it were not for him, the gang that attacked my madrasa would surely have destroyed it."

"What?"

"Yes, it's true! We are indebted to him—Khoja Hoseyn says the reason that other gang fought them off was because he pays protection money for the whole neighborhood. Isn't that generous of him?" Ali Baba smiles and leaves the kitchen.

I'm stunned. None of it makes sense. I can't keep my mind on my work and must see this man with my own eyes. When it's time for Jamal to serve the food, I put on my scarf and drape it over my face before helping my brother carry the dishes out to the men.

Ali Baba's guest is lanky, with a surprisingly large belly for one so otherwise slender. He has dark eyes, and his high cheekbones are almost hidden under a thick, bushy white beard. Almost, but not quite. The blood drains from my face. My body freezes as I remember the face of the devil-man standing over Abu-Zayed. It's true he's always been in shadow when I've seen him, but the shape of his face seems so familiar in my mind. Something about this man . . . Could this Khoja Hoseyn be the captain of the Forty Thieves?

I bite my lip and try not to stare. Before I can pull my eyes away, I notice the shape of a dagger hidden under his garments. A friendly guest would never arm himself before dining with a host. He intends to kill Ali Baba and Rasheed after he enjoys their hospitality!

I shake like a spring leaf as I usher Jamal around the partition where the washing basin and linens are kept.

He slips his hand into mine, looking as if he's seen a demon.

"Jamal—"

He nods his head, his eyes wide. "It's him!"

I draw him close. "I know. Ali Baba's guest is really—"

"Red Beard!" Jamal whispers.

"What? No." I kneel down beside him. "Not Red Beard. This man is really the captain of the Forty—" I stop. Red Beard. Could it be? I peek around the partition at the men and picture the merchant with a bright red beard and darkened eyes. I almost gasp out loud. Jamal is right! And so am I. The devil-man and the leader of the gangs are the same man. That's why Red Beard calls up some of his older gang members to replace his men—men in his band of Forty Thieves! And to think that little Jamal sat with him on his horse and hoped to be just like him!

We can't leave Khoja Hoseyn alone with the men after supper. I take hold of Jamal's arms and give him a grave look. "Jamal, this man is not just Red Beard.

He's the captain of the thieves who killed the guards and kidnapped us. He killed Master and tried to kill Ali Baba and Rasheed! If we don't do something, he'll try it again tonight!"

Jamal's lip trembles.

"Remember how we were brave enough to escape him in the desert? Now, don't be afraid to go back in there. You're a bold warrior. Red Beard thought so himself, didn't he?"

He nods. "But when he sees me, he'll be mad I ran away from him those times. What if he—"

"Remember, he's not after you; he's after them because they know the secret of the cave."

"So do I!"

"But he doesn't know that. You need to go back out there and pretend you don't know any of this. Pretend you don't even recognize him. I know you can do it, Jamal. I have a plan to warn Ali Baba and Rasheed who Khoja really is, but I need you to be brave like Sinbad, from Rasheed's stories. Can you do that, little donkey?"

Jamal nods.

I give him a hug. "I'll be back soon."

While Jamal attends to the men, I slip to my room and fasten the silver dagger's sheath around my thigh.

"Marjana!"

I jump at Saja's voice from the window. "You startled me!" I help her into the room. "My nerves are hopping like hot grease over fire—I'm glad you're here."

"I wanted to give you this." Saja holds something between her fingers.

I smile as she places it in my palm.

"Sesame. 'You are my treasure.'"

Such a tiny seed for such an ocean of feelings. I slip my knife from its sheath and open the hidden compartment at the end of the dagger's hilt, dropping the seed into the secret place with the sprig of jasmine. "I'll keep it near me always." I shut the lid and slide the knife back into the sheath.

"But, Saja, something awful has happened." I tell her the news. The blood drains from Saja's face when she hears the captain of the Forty Thieves is Red Beard and that he's in the house this very moment. I take her by the elbow. "I need your help."

Her eyes grow wide. "I can't do anything to stop him!"

"I have a plan for when the men are finished eating, but Saja, I need you to go get the magistrate."

"Alone? The magistrate's far from the bathhouse—" She glances nervously at me. "I could use one of Ali Baba's mules, but it's getting so dark!" She wrings her hands. "Will the magistrate even listen to me?" She bites her lip. "I'll make him listen. But what if the mistress of the baths finds out?" She takes in a sharp breath. "What if the captain gets away and finds out?"

"I know you can do it. You saved me from the boy with the club. You can do this. We have to stop Red Beard from being a danger to any more boys like Badi."

Saja stares at me with wide eyes. Finally, she takes a deep breath and nods. "I will." The words seem to give her strength like some kind of strange magic, and she stands up straighter. "I will."

"Be careful!" I hug her before helping her out the window and watch her disappear into the night. My treasure.

When I rush back to Jamal, he's almost done collecting the dishes. We have to keep the devil-man from being alone with the men for as long as possible until Saja brings the magistrate. I pull Jamal aside and hand him his pipe and tabor. "Here! Walk into the room ahead of me, playing. It's part of the plan."

Jamal frowns. "But we weren't invited. And how can dancing and music be a good plan?"

"Well, who would have thought that something as simple as storytelling could be such a powerful plan? But it worked for Scheherazade in Rasheed's tales, didn't it?" I try to keep my voice pleasant so I won't frighten him. "Remember what Rasheed said—music is existence itself. And the Sufis' whirling dance brings them closer to Allah. Our music and dancing can be powerful, too."

Jamal stands up straighter and tucks the drum under his arm.

I pull the veil of my headdress down over my eyes so the captain won't recognize me. "Let's make it strong and beautiful."

Jamal nods and begins beating the drum and playing the pipe as he walks into the room, announcing our presence. We wait, silently, for permission to continue.

Khoja Hoseyn's smile fades when he sees us, but when Ali Baba claps in appreciation, he pretends to be pleased and claps as well. The devil-man stares hard at Jamal and me but doesn't say a word. I curtsy and Jamal bows.

"Ah, Khoja," Ali Baba says to him, "you shall have some delightful entertainment. Our young friends are extremely talented. Please, children, proceed."

And then we begin. The old, familiar sound of my brother's drumming moves my hands first, starting from the tips of my fingers. My hands dance for my audience, who watch, mesmerized, as my fingers curl and sway and beckon to them like trees in the wind. Their eyes grow larger and they lean in closer. They never knew fingers could dance all by themselves. Their hands don't know how to do such things. They watch as my arms join the dance, and slowly, slowly, my shoulders, my hips, my feet. All to Jamal's beat.

My dancing hands and his drumming hands have always been connected by an invisible magic thread. We always know what each other needs during the dance without saying a word. Soon, the beat moves from my limbs to my heart, waking my strength and courage. My whole body comes alive. Jamal has never played so well. His bravery speaks through every beat.

After several dances, I draw my dagger from its sheath for my final performance and make a graceful pass as I leap through the air. I use the dagger as a dramatic prop and lunge toward the men as if to attack, pretending to be a ruthless robber with a sword. Jamal catches on quickly to my new dance and intensifies his rhythm.

I point the blade to Rasheed's breast, then spin toward Ali Baba. As I draw near to Ali Baba, I try to alert him with my eyes as well as my actions, glancing pointedly toward Khoja Hoseyn and back to Ali Baba. I raise my knife to Ali Baba's throat before spinning away.

The feverish beat of the drum and my movements seem to set my whole body on fire. My heart beats harder than it ever has before. Finally, I'm so exhausted I can dance no longer. But I have to make Ali Baba understand so he can defend himself. Out of breath, my chest heaving, I grab Jamal's tabor. With my dagger poised above Ali Baba, I flip the drum over and hold it out to him as if I'm a robber demanding money from a victim. I pray he understands my warnings about the devil-man.

But Ali Baba and Rasheed merely chuckle and drop some dinars into the drum.

My heart sinks like a stone.

The captain, on the other hand, seems to understand my message perfectly. Out of the corner of my eye, I see the captain's hand slide toward his own dagger, hidden beneath his robe. The men are not alarmed, thinking their guest is also reaching for his purse to give me a present. They don't notice the fierce gleam in his eyes.

I can't wait any longer for Saja and the magistrate.

Swallowing my fear, I spin toward the captain. The devil-man's fingers wrap around the hilt of his knife, and a glint of metal flashes as it parts from its sheath.

He lunges toward Ali Baba.

26

"No!" I cry, and jump between Ali Baba and the devil-man. My body and the captain's slam together like two rushing winds; only my knife separates us. It plunges deep into his belly, and the devil-man falls to the floor as I draw the bloody dagger from his body.

The room spins.

Ali Baba leaps to his feet. "Oh, Marjana!" he cries. He and Rasheed stare in horror at the fallen guest.

Breathless, I kick the captain's dagger out of reach and stand over him as he holds his wound and gasps for breath.

The devil-man looks up at me. I've lost my veil in the confusion. His expression is full of fire, until he sees my eyes. "Khubz." The devil-man's eyes slide shut, and a strangled laugh escapes his throat. "So my fortune has come true. I shall 'die by the sword of one who is not what they were.'" He stares back up at me and chokes out another harsh laugh.

With one last effort, the captain reaches toward the drum that fell nearby and scrapes Ali Baba's gold coins into his palm. His fingers close around them as he takes his last breath. His body falls limp.

Alarmed at my cry, Mistress and Leila run into the room. Their faces are white with fear. Loud voices ring out from the front of the house. Fists bang open the door. The magistrate and his men burst into the room, Saja at their side. "What is the meaning of this?" the magistrate demands, glancing at the body.

Ali Baba rushes to my side. "Are you all right? Marjana, I don't understand—what's happened?"

My dagger slips from my trembling fingers and

clatters to the floor. I struggle to catch my breath.

Saja hurries to me. "Praise Allah, you're safe!" Bending over the dead man, Saja pulls off his false white beard and lifts his garments, exposing the padding of his disguise. "Ali Baba, the magistrate has come for this man—Marjana saved you from a murderer!"

Ali Baba looks stunned. The magistrate's eyebrows rise at the sight of the green serpent on the devil-man's chest.

I finally find my voice. "Ali Baba, you've entertained your enemy—not only was Khoja Hoseyn your neighbor and the oil merchant, he was also Red Beard, leader of the gangs, *and* the captain of the Forty Thieves!"

Ali Baba puts his arm around Leila and draws her near. They stare at me in astonishment. Mistress gives an anguished sob.

The magistrate's eyes grow wide. "It's true. Praise Allah! We've been trying to stop this man for years!"

I lift the dining cloth from the floor, and Saja helps me cover the captain's body.

"Take him away!" the magistrate yells to his men. As

they carry the body away, he bows to Saja and me. "May Allah bless you both. This is a night of rejoicing for the city of Baghdad." He turns to Ali Baba, beaming. "It looks as if the reward money you so generously offered shall be given to this young woman's master, sir." He gestures to Saja. "Since she reported the captain's whereabouts directly to me."

"Certainly," Ali Baba whispers, as if still in shock. "I will give it to her master myself. The reward is worth at least four times her bond—I will make certain he grants her freedom and provides for her as well."

The magistrate bows again to Saja before leaving. Her mouth falls open in disbelief as she watches him go. When she turns to me, her face shines like the sun.

Jamal, who had been silent, runs to me and flings his arms around my waist. "You saved us. Just like Scheherazade!"

I hug him tightly as the room slowly stops spinning. "With your help, little donkey!" I sink to my knees beside Rasheed. He takes my hand as the truth of what has happened slowly dawns on us all.

Rasheed shakes his head in amazement. "I have a good imagination, but I could never have imagined the wonderful places fate would take me or my family. It's been like an incredible magic carpet ride." He hands me my knife. "I'm grateful fate brought you to us."

Leila drops beside me and clasps my other hand. "Yes, praise Allah."

Ali Baba throws his hands up in wonder. "I have been a fool, and you have saved us yet again."

I shake my head. "No, Ali Baba. Your good heart sometimes blinds you to others' wickedness, but you are not a fool."

He shakes his head. "I hardly know what to say." A look passes between him and Leila, and Ali Baba speaks. "It would be our honor to have you and your brother join our family if this pleases you. Not as servants, but as dear friends. Of course, for so long, we did not have much to share, but now there is the entire treasure cave to share with as many people as we want!"

My mouth falls open and I don't even care that my scarf is gone.

Saja beams at me and squeezes my shoulder. I hold my knife with the secret of Saja's sesame seed and Umi's sweet jasmine hidden in its hilt. I almost laugh out loud from the joy that bubbles to my heart. First Saja's friendship, and now a family. That day so long ago when the devil-man and his thieves stole Jamal and me away, I never would have imagined my fate held such riches. When Abu-Zayed spoke as the storyteller, he was right about the threads of fate being woven in such an intricate, beautiful way. Umi would be pleased.

The thought of becoming a member of a loving family makes me feel as if I'm standing in front of my own magic treasure cave where all I have to say is something as simple as "Open, Sesame" and it will be mine.

Ali Baba pulls Jamal near and ruffles his hair. My brother grins up at him, and a sense of peace fills my soul. I stare down at the hands cradling mine. They feel warm and strong.

Ali Baba clears his throat and looks anxiously at me. "Will you?" he asks.

A thousand jinn could not stop me from being a part of something so wonderful and true. I glance at Saja's bright face and gaze into the eyes of Ali Baba and his family.

"Yes." I smile as I speak my very own magic words. "I will."

Author's Note

I first heard the exciting story of "Ali Baba and the Forty Thieves" as a child, listening to a collection of audio recordings from *The Arabian Nights*. It was my favorite of the tales, and daring young Marjana never ceased to intrigue me. Around that time, my father took my brother and me to see the film *Gandhi*, starring Ben Kingsley, which had a lasting impression on me. Afterward, the kind, unassuming voice of Ali Baba from the audiotapes was forever paired in my mind with Kingsley's image of soft-spoken Gandhi, and most likely influenced my idea of making Ali Baba a peaceful humanitarian, who gave away his treasure instead of keeping it for himself.

The Arabian Nights, or *The Thousand and One Nights*, is part of both Arabic and European literature and is a jumble of narratives—epics, fairy tales, fables, comedies, political works, and more—some of which have roots in Sanskrit, Persian, and Greek literature. The tales are framed around a central story of a young woman named Scheherazade, who volunteers to marry a king who murders a new wife every night. Each evening, Scheherazade ends her tales on such cliff-hangers that he keeps her alive in order to hear what happens next. In this way, the thousand and one stories save her life and the lives of countless other women.

An important and recurring theme throughout the *Nights* tales is the idea of predestination and the relationship between free will and fate. Arabic folklore abounds with proverbs extoling the power of fate, such as *What is written will be fulfilled*, which literally means *What is written on the forehead must be seen by the eye*. Many protagonists of *The Arabian Nights* tales set out to beat fate but find that their evasive actions actually become the very vehicle that fate uses to bring about their destiny, just like in Abu-Zayed's story about the man trying to trick death. Marjana sees fate as a wind blowing toward a certain destination, while Master seeks to avoid his fate by sneaking away to the cave and stealing the treasure. He ends up losing everything, just as the fortune-teller Abu-Zayed predicted.

Marjana's story takes place in the mid-tenth century CE, when the Buyids had taken control of medieval Baghdad from the Abbasids, and it was an increasingly lawless city. During this time, it was home to a vast counterculture of street folk. Beggars, pickpockets, treasure hunters, musicians, comedians, mimics, snake charmers, sorcerers, swindlers, and storytellers crowded the busy markets, all desperately surviving by means of their wits and wiles.

Around this period, territorial bands of ruffians and vagabonds called ayyarun also plagued the streets. These armed gangs collected money from area merchants in exchange for protection from rival gangs. Their leaders really did ride on each other's backs and used helmets, shields, and harnesses woven from plaited palm leaves.

Tucked inside this rough-and-tumble setting lies

another historical reality of Marjana's world; in the medieval Middle East, women moved in a sphere completely separate from men. The harem is the best illustration of the sharp divide between the genders. All wives in a household lived in a separated section of the home with their young children and extended female relations, servants, and slaves, forming a close, sometimes complex community. Male khādim guards, eunuchs, also lived in the harems to protect the women and children and to keep a close eye on them. Marriage was not usually seen as a romantic union between a man and a woman but a matter of property transfer from the father to the groom, who acquired the woman to begin his own familial line.

Though women were generally discouraged from stepping outside these bounds, there existed subcultures within the broad, rich culture of the medieval Middle East that offered alternative perspectives on women's roles. During the time of our story, there was a growing movement of Muslim mystics called Sufis who sought to experience the spiritual reality behind their religious texts and rituals and grow closer to Allah through spiritual learning known as tariqa. Sufism, known as tasawwuf in the Arabic-speaking world, continues to be practiced by many Muslim worshipers today.

As Rasheed tells Marjana, Sufis practice meditation, rhythmic movement, music, and chanting to open their hearts to the divine and to connect with Allah. Like Ali Baba's family, Sufis emphasize the unity in nature and devote their lives to meditation and devotion to Allah and to an existence free from worldly gain. Sufis advise respect and honor for the feminine and integrate women in their ceremonies, valuing them as active participants.

Eighth-century Sufi Rabi'a al-'Adawiyya of Basra is one example of the many celebrated women in the history of the movement. As a child, Rabi'a was sold into slavery and freed herself from a cruel master through her faith in Allah. Later in life, she chose not to marry in order to devote herself to God. Rabi'a is remembered as one of the greatest Sufis in Islam.

Another intriguing subculture involved the Safavid women from Iran. Their "soul sister" vows were common in the sixteenth century, and I wanted to include this fascinating ritualistic union among two female best friends in my tenth-century story. These unions were considered vital and were recognized and fostered by the entire community.

Ali Baba's wife, Leila, mentions several actual ways in which these kindred spirits communicated their most intimate moods and feelings using kitchen supplies as secret gifts with coded meanings, though I have altered their meanings slightly for the sake of the story I wanted to tell. The vow of sisterhood entailed a fierce loyalty and was often displayed by dressing alike, moving in the same social circles, not talking about each other behind one another's back, and even inheriting property. The engagement involved a sort of matchmaker, a reputable woman who arranged the union just as Leila describes it in the story. The couple then visited a shrine on a religious holiday to make their union public. One woman would declare, "In the name of Ali, the Shah-conqueror of Khaybar," and the other would reply, "Oh God, accept and fulfill our desire." Afterward, there was celebrating with dancing and drinking of sherbert.

While these historical pictures of medieval Middle Eastern women are refreshing and complex, female characters in *The Arabian Nights* tales are generally confined to two strict categories: dangerous women, such as witches and adulteresses, or safe women—devout, sensible creatures who are merely decorative to the plot. The slave girl Marjana, however, seems to possess both the bold, passionate characteristics of the former and the loyalty and integrity of the latter.

As a dancer, Marjana possesses an energy and vivaciousness. She certainly embodies boldness, taking over Ali Baba's mess, patching up his brother's mishap, diverting the robbers, then incapacitating them when they showed up later, and finally saving Ali Baba and his son from the captain. No one could deny Marjana's fierce loyalty. But what are her motivations? *Why* is she so passionate and brave? What could possibly provoke a slave to risk her life more than once for the sake of a new master?

Since the traditional tale never gives us the answers to these questions and relegates Marjana, the natural choice for the leading role, to the background, I thought it time to pull this fascinating young woman into the limelight and let her shine.

Acknowledgments

I would like to thank Charlie Ilgunas for his enthusiastic collaboration and hard work on this project. I am also grateful for the constructive words of encouragement and critique provided by readers Anne Marie Pace, Francoise Bui, Erin Murphy, Alex Lenzi, Elizabeth Reimer, and Jennifer Duddy Gill, with a special appreciation for the insights and guidance of Tasneem Daud.

Thank you to *Hunger Mountain VCFA Journal for the Arts* for awarding the middle grade category of the Katherine Paterson Prize in 2011 to an excerpt of an early version of *The Forty Thieves*, and to the *Lascaux Review* for awarding it the Eldin Fellowship in 2015. I would also like to acknowledge the folks at Cricket Magazine Group for first publishing a shorter, serialized version of *The Forty Thieves* in *Cricket* magazine in 2016.

Finally, I want to express my heartfelt gratitude to my family for their enduring love and support.